"I've never said that to another woman!"

Kai's eyes flashed in anger. "I love you, Faye. What the hell is wrong with that?"

Faye's heart was pounding and there was a lump in her throat, an ache inside her. "Nothing. Only...only I don't want to get in over my head... and drown."

"What makes you think you'll drown?" he asked, puzzled.

Her body went rigid, her nerves taut. Faye turned away from him. "I know I would," she said flatly. "I just know it."

If she should give in, if ever she should admit she loved him—to herself, to him—only heartbreak would come of it. She could never be the kind of wife he wanted. No, she could never marry Kai. Nor could she ever tell him why!

KAREN VAN DER ZEE

a secret sorrow

Harlequin Books

TORONTO • LONDON • LOS ANGELES • AMSTERDAM
SYDNEY • HAMBURG • PARIS • STOCKHOLM • ATHENS • TOKYO

Harlequin Presents edition published June 1981
ISBN 0-373-10433-2

Original hardcover edition published in 1981
by Mills & Boon Limited

CHAPTER ONE

NUMB with shock, Faye stared at the doctor. It wasn't possible that she had heard it right. It *couldn't* be true! Not once in those terrifying weeks of her hospitalisation had this possibility occurred to her. But the doctor sitting behind his desk was no product of her imagination and neither were the words he had spoken. His eyes were very kind and full of compassion, and Faye couldn't bear to look at him. No one had ever looked at her quite like that.

'No,' she whispered. 'No.' She closed her eyes. Oh, God, she thought. *No! No!*

Silence was the only answer. Doctor Martin was watching her, she could feel his gaze almost like a physical touch. She looked up and met his eyes.

'You're sure? You're absolutely sure?'

He nodded slowly. 'I'm afraid so.'

Why had she asked? It was a stupid question. She knew her biology, the basics at least, and that was all that was required to understand the cold reality. It was basic, simple, and totally devastating. Everything inside her screamed out in revolt.

'Why didn't you tell me before?' she cried. 'Why didn't anybody tell me before?' Her voice sounded strange in her own ears, pitched with near hysteria.

'You're a fighter, Faye, in mind and in body, but you needed every ounce of your strength to stay alive. Had I told you while you were still in the hospital it might have broken your spirit.' He spoke slowly, his voice gentle. 'It was too risky, Faye. I had to wait until you were all better so you'd be able to cope with this without giving up altogether.'

'But now that I'm better, I'll just laugh it off? Is

that what you're thinking? It won't break my spirit now? I'll live happily ever after as if it makes no difference?'

He didn't seem to take offence at her accusing tone, as though he understood that she had to let out the agony that filled her being. His eyes, still kind and sympathetic, didn't leave her face.

'It will make all the difference in the world,' he said quietly, 'for the rest of your life. But you're in fine physical shape now and you'll probably live to be a healthy hundred. I think that your spirit and your willpower will see you through this crisis. It won't be easy to adjust, and it will take time, but you'll make it, I'm sure.'

It was easy for him to be so sure, she thought in wild, hot anger. Everybody always had such confidence in competent, reliable, self-sufficient Faye Sherwood. Faye would make it. Faye would manage. Faye could cope with anything. But this time she herself was not so sure.

'Fae,' the doctor said after a slight pause, 'I'll speak to your fiancé if you like.'

Greg.

With desperate strength Faye suppressed a burst of hysterical laughter. Greg would probably be delighted when he heard the news. What she thought of as a disaster, he'd consider a welcome convenience. It would fit in with his plans just right.

She was shocked, suddenly, by the bitter sarcasm of her thoughts, and a wave of guilt surged through her. How could she think of Greg that way after all he had gone through with her in those past months? His daily visits, the gifts of flowers and books, his constant attention had helped her through the most frightening time of her life.

'He's ... he's in Los Angeles right now, but when he comes back I'll tell him myself.' Somehow she didn't think it would be so difficult. She pushed her chair back and stood up. 'Thank you, Doctor.'

He motioned to the chair. 'Please sit down. There's one more thing I need to say.'

Faye did as he requested and watched him as he pulled a prescription pad towards him and quickly wrote something down. She jerked upright.

'I don't want any tranquillisers!'

Doctor Martin smiled, looking at her with warm humour in his eyes. 'See, just as I thought—ready to fight!' He tore off the paper and handed it to her. 'No tranquillisers. This is the name of a doctor I'd like you to see a few times—Doctor Jaworski. He'll help guide your fighting spirit in the right direction.'

Faye took the slip of paper and stared at the name: Nathan Jaworski. She swallowed. 'Is he a psychiatrist? A therapist of some sort?'

Doctor Martin nodded. 'He does a lot of work with people who are mourning the loss of a loved one—a husband or a child, or the loss of part of their own bodies—a leg, an arm. And also with people who are dying and have to adjust to the inevitable.' He paused and played with his pen. 'When you're grieving you go through a more or less predictable series of emotions—denial, rage, depression, and finally acceptance. You will too, Faye. In the end you will learn to accept.'

Carefully Faye folded the paper and slipped it in her wallet behind her credit cards and driver's licence. She hadn't lost a husband, or a leg, and she wasn't going to die. She would have to think about going to Doctor Jaworski.

She took a deep breath and rose to her feet once more.

'Thank you, Doctor,' she said automatically, and managed a polite little smile. *Thank you, Doctor, for the worst news of my life.*

'I'm not sure you should be driving by yourself,' he said carefully. 'Shall I call someone to come and get you? A relative? A friend?'

He didn't trust her state of mind, Faye could tell. Did he think she might jump off a bridge? Or end up in another car crash and get her head bashed in this time?

'Thank you, no, I'll be all right. My car is at the office; I came here on foot. It's such a beautiful day. . . .'

Such a beautiful day. . . . As Faye walked back to her office she wondered how a day like this could happen in February. It was like spring—bright, clean and almost warm. It seemed that everyone in Chicago was out enjoying the sun. The benches in the little park near her office were all occupied. Old people staring off into space, mothers with their children, a big pregnant woman, belly way out in proud demonstration, face upward to catch the sun. There were infants everywhere, in baby carriages and strollers, bundled up in snowsuits, like little cocoons, their tiny faces barely exposed.

She wanted to scream. Children. I'll never have children, she thought. I'll never waddle around with a big belly worrying if I'll ever get my shape back. I'll never be a mother, never nurse a baby. The tears came then, blinding her, blurring everything around her until she saw nothing but a swirling mixture of colours and shapes. I wish I were dead, she thought.

But not so long ago she hadn't wanted to die. With everything in her she had fought to stay alive as she lay in the intensive care unit of the hospital where they had taken her after the accident. 'Critical condition,' 'massive abdominal injuries,' were two of the terms that had been used in the newspaper report. Somebody with too much alcohol in his system had crashed into her as he came flying around the corner on the wrong side of the road. A head-on collision, a nightmare she had wanted to forget. But now she would never forget, because it would be with her every day of her life. It would change everything, her whole future, her entire life.

The traffic light was red. She waited at the curb for it to change, feeling the breeze cold on her wet cheeks, faintly aware of people staring at her. She felt freezing cold and a shudder ran through her and then another and another. She wanted to scream out in bitter anguish, but her throat was thick with sobs and no sound came.

Faye took the bath towel off and looked at herself in the mirror. She looked at herself often these days. Ever since she had talked to Doctor Martin five weeks ago she had had a strange fascination for her body—for her flat stomach with the pink scars.

Moisture from her shower still clung to her skin and from under the towel wrapped around her hair drops of water dripped on to her shoulders. Too tall, too skinny, too many freckles. Her stomach was flat—flat for ever. Barren, she thought unemotionally. I'm a barren woman. Wasn't that what they called it in the Bible? A word with a stigma. A woman incomplete, defective, deficient.

She stared blindly at the mirror, feeling emotion flooding back, overwhelming her again. Would it always be like that? Would she never be able to think about it without hurting so much? She felt broken, mutilated, incomplete, a feeling that tore at the very roots of her femininity. It was a primitive, instinctive emotion, and she seemed to have no control over it. She had tried, she had tried so hard in those last few weeks, but it only seemed to be getting worse.

And now she was here, in Connecticut, with her brother and his two children, fresh off the plane this very afternoon, in a last desperate attempt to start over—To Start a New Life.

And it seemed as if nature was trying to encourage her, showing its new life in brightly coloured crocuses and daffodils blooming everywhere in this small Connecticut town of New Canaan. And Faye had noticed it. As they had driven to Chuck's home through the beautiful winding roads she had seen the flowers, the fresh green grass, the forsythias bursting into golden bloom. Spring, she'd thought. New life and colour and warmth, and I feel dead.

Faye shivered and wrapped the towel back around her body. She had to keep trying. She couldn't give in to the numb, grey, mindless depression that had held her in its grip those last few weeks.

She had thought that the accident and the weeks in the hospital had been nothing short of a nightmare, but the real torment had not begun until after that fateful visit to Doctor Martin's office. She couldn't function any more. At work she would blindly stare at the papers in front of her, not knowing whether it was English or French or Spanish she was reading; not knowing whether she was supposed to do a rewrite or a translation. At night she would struggle awake out of unremembered dreams, her face and pillow wet.

A week later she was no longer employed and no longer engaged. Her mother had come to Faye's city apartment, taken one look at her and taken her back home to the suburbs. Faye had gone without protest. She didn't care. Nothing mattered.

Settled in her old room, she didn't want to get out of bed, even though she hardly slept. She didn't want to eat. Her mother hovered over her in despair with soft-boiled eggs and bowls of homemade chicken soup. The house was full of the fragrances of baking bread and simmering stews, but nothing at all could tempt her appetite.

Her father, normally a quiet man, began talking to her, attempting to draw her into discussions about political or social issues. But Faye was not interested, although usually she was. Nothing seemed important any more.

Her rational mind told her she should do something, make a new start in life, reorganise her priorities, make different plans for the future, but she didn't know how or where to begin, so she did nothing. She lay in bed with eyes open, seeing nothing. She just wanted to lie there and drift away into nothingness. She didn't want to think or feel and inside her there was nothing but a dull grey bleakness, and maybe even that would eventually leave her.

Then her brother Chuck came to Chicago with his two children for a visit, expecting to find her well and happy. Instead they found her in bed, looking ill and miserable. She was unresponsive and not at all her usual warm, loving self. Darci and Joey, only six and eight, were terrified, the memory of their mother's death still easily recalled. They pleaded with Faye not to die, as if it were up to her. She was supposed to be *better*, Daddy had *told* them so. Daddy had promised them Auntie Faye wasn't going to die, like Mommy had.

'I'm not going to die,' she promised them. 'I'm not sick, just a little tired and upset.' Somehow their tearful voices and frightened little faces touched off deep inside her a spark of feeling, a glimmer of life.

'Come home with us,' Chuck offered one morning. 'We'd love to have you. Maybe you should try and get a job in New York. A change would do you good.'

Everybody was feeling sorry for her, but for the wrong reasons. Her depression was due to her broken engagement, or so they thought, and she'd left her job to avoid seeing Greg every day. It wasn't true, but it was convenient to let them believe it, because she wasn't ready to tell them the real reason yet. Maybe she never would. The only one she had told was Greg.

Faye shivered again and opened up her suitcases to find her robe and hairdryer. The house was very quiet. As soon as they had come home Darci and Joey had wanted to go see their maternal grandparents who lived down the road to tell them all about Chicago. Faye had stayed behind to wash away a glass of Coke that Darci had spilled all over her in the plane.

'We won't be long,' Chuck had said, but when Faye heard a noise in the house she wondered how it was possible to make a visit in less than fifteen minutes. Someone was walking around in the house, but she didn't hear the children and being that quiet was alien to their natures. She slipped on the short terrycloth robe and grimaced at the mirror when she saw the green colour clash painfully with the purple towel wrapped around her hair. She went into the hall and down the stairs.

'Chuck? Is that you?' she called, and walked into the living room.

It wasn't.

She stopped dead in her tracks and stared. A man sat stretched out in a chair, feet up on an ottoman, glass in hand. He looked at her with eyes so blue they dazzled her. Never before had she seen eyes that bright. His blond hair was bleached almost white, his tan so deep and dark, it most certainly hadn't been acquired locally. Another quick glance took in the long legs covered with jeans tucked into knee-high leather boots, a black turtleneck sweater, and again the bright blue eyes that seemed to draw her like magnets. Who was he? Paul Newman's younger brother?

He seemed totally at ease and not at all taken aback by her appearance. He smiled at her, showing dazzling white teeth, and raised his glass.

'Howdy, ma'am!' he said, and took a drink from his

glass. His tone was a slow, lazy drawl, originating somewhere deep down South, Faye knew.

'Make yourself at home,' she answered coolly, piqued by the thought that he behaved as if he belonged there, sitting in her brother's chair with a drink in his hand.

He grinned widely. 'Why, thank you, ma'am,' he drawled, inclining his head. Then, slowly sipping from his glass, he let his gaze travel over her body, top to toes, a curious sparkle in his eyes. 'Glad to see Chuck finally got himself another woman. Was about time.'

It took a minute for his words to sink in. 'I'm *not* his woman!' she managed finally, her tone acid.

His face fell and he looked disappointed. 'That's too bad. He's becoming a monk and he needs a woman in his life.'

The man annoyed her with his conclusions about what Chuck should or shouldn't need, and she was about to turn and leave him where he was when he smiled at her again.

'Pardon my asking, ma'am, but who are you, if not Chuck's new love?'

'I'm his *sister*!'

'Interesting, very interesting.' His lazy tone and the laughter in his eyes deepened her irritation.

'Isn't it?'

'That look of yours gives me frostbite,' he commented calmly. 'What's the matter? Don't you like me?'

'Should I?'

'You wouldn't be the first. It's known to have happened before.'

She didn't doubt it. Playboy of the year if she ever saw one. He hadn't got that tan sitting behind a desk working, like most of humanity in these parts. He looked as if he'd been skiing in Colorado, or lying on a beach in Florida. She looked at him coldly. 'I'll take my time making up my mind. Fortunately for you my first impressions have sometimes been wrong—in a few isolated cases.'

He whistled between his teeth in mock admiration. 'Calm, quiet Chuck got himself a real fiery sister,' he said softly.

He moved his left hand on to his thigh and Faye's eyes caught the bandage around the wrist, stark white against the deep tan of his skin.

'Did you do that skiing?' she asked, motioning towards the bandaged wrist. 'Or did somebody trip over you while you were asleep on the beach?' The contempt in her voice was intentional, but as she heard her own tone she wondered what had got into her to talk like that to a stranger.

The man in the chair didn't seem to be perturbed in the least and the mockery in his eyes made it clear that he knew her thoughts.

'No, ma'am,' he said politely. 'Just a minor little accident while I was frolicking in Kano.'

'Kano?' she asked coolly, raising her brows.

The blue eyes were brilliant with undisguised humour. 'Kano—Northern Nigeria,' he explained. 'Peanuts, rice, sorghum and lots of lovely irrigation systems.'

Shame welled up inside her. She had been acting like a perfect bitch, jumping to conclusions. He'd acquired the tan working, and even if he hadn't, it was none of her business. It might have been his first vacation in years, what did she know?

Nothing. Not even his name. A perfect stranger sitting in her brother's house, drinking her brother's Scotch while she was walking around the house undressed, thinking she was alone.

'Would you mind telling me who you are?' she

asked, her voice chilly. 'For all I know you could have walked in here off the street. . . .'

'. . . planning to take off with the silver,' he finished for her in his lazy drawl.

'Right you are,' she said with cool hauteur.

Texas, she thought, no doubt it was a Texas accent, and suddenly something strange happened in her mind. She remembered things the children had told her, and odds and ends of information tucked away in her mind began to take on a new significance. It was as if the pieces of a puzzle were coming together making a picture totally different from what she had visualised. This man couldn't be . . .

'Kai's the name, ma'am. Kai Ellington.'

It was. *Uncle* Kai, the children called him, a hero in their eyes. The man who had flown them to Disney World in Florida last summer, stayed there with them for a week to give Chuck a reprieve and rest from single fatherhood. He was the man who took them on camping trips, to the Brooklyn Zoo and the Barnum and Bailey Circus in New York. Faye swallowed with difficulty, feeling suddenly small and dumb. This man was Chuck's best friend, the man who had been his partner and still now shared Chuck's home office with him. That was how he had entered the house, she realised, through the office adjoining the living room.

For some reason she had expected this 'Uncle Kai' to be short and balding, shy and woman-wary, a bachelor in his middle thirties afraid of matrimony. A sugar daddy with more money than sex appeal.

A helpless laugh almost escaped her, but she suppressed it with difficulty. When God passed out sex appeal, Kai Ellington had stood in line twice!

Leaning comfortably back in his chair, he was looking at her with unconcealed appraisal and she became suddenly aware of what he must be seeing. Her toes curled into the thick carpeting and she closed her robe tighter around her. She looked terrible in that green thing and that purple towel around her hair. She had taken the towel from the top of the pile in the closet and had figured it must be Joey's when she saw the Incredible Hulk sprawling all over it in sickening green.

'Freckles,' he commented after a moment's silence, as if that made up the sum total of her appearance.

'Very observant!'

'Hundreds of them,' he continued.

'Don't remind me,' she said coldly.

One eyebrow lifted. 'You're not too pleased with them, I take it?' His smile was charming. 'I for one happen to like freckles. Adds character to a face, a touch of spice.'

She had never heard that one before, she had to admit. Was it a sincere compliment or just mindless mockery? His eyes didn't leave her face.

'And that lovely purple towel hides a headful of red hair.'

'Your powers of deduction are quite amazing,' she said sarcastically, wondering why she was still standing there submitting herself to his scrutiny.

'But your eyes,' he drawled, 'they're brown. Aren't they supposed to be green?'

'I'm sorry you don't approve, but Mother Nature had an off-day when she assembled me.'

His laugh was hearty and infectious and she couldn't help smiling a little.

'I'm glad. That makes you an original. I never did like assembly-line art.'

He himself wasn't made up from a ready-made kit, either, Faye thought, remembering things Chuck and the kids had told her. *Kai* for one wasn't what you'd call an ordinary name. He had been named after a Chinese friend of his father's. He looked like a Viking, and he came from Texas—a more odd assortment of facts she couldn't imagine.

'Sit down, have a drink,' he said suddenly, as if he owned the place.

'No, thanks, I'd better get dressed.' She turned and walked back to her room where she unwound the Incredible Hulk from around her head and began to dry her hair. She was lucky, she thought. Wash 'n wear hair. Thick, short and curly, it never needed setting. Seven, eight minutes with her blowdryer and presto! it was ready to face the world. As she was applying mascara, she heard the phone ring and dashing from the room she went in search of it, only to find that Kai was answering it, leaning against the kitchen wall with easy grace. Standing there he looked even taller than she had thought him to be, with broad shoulders and lean hips. His boots seemed to accentuate his long, strong legs and his whole appearance was one of vitality and virile masculinity.

From the conversation she gathered that it was Chuck calling, and it angered her that Kai made no motions to hand over the receiver to her. She was standing there, waiting, and he was looking right at her.

'She's not ready yet,' she heard him say as he flicked a glance along her body still clad in the green robe. 'And I have a better idea, I'll take her out to dinner.' Laughter followed in response to something Chuck was saying. 'Okay, fine, I'll see you tomorrow.' He replaced the receiver and smiled at her.

'Lovely red hair,' he said slowly. 'Just the way I thought it would look.'

Faye ignored the compliment. 'That phone call was for *me*!' she said icily.

He shrugged easily. 'I took care of it, I thought you were dressing. Besides, it was only Chuck. He wanted to know if you were ready so he could pick you up.

His parents-in-law invited all of you to stay for dinner.'

'I'd like to go! What makes you think I want to go out to dinner with *you*?'

There was a short silence and he observed her with sudden serious contemplation.

'We'll be seeing a lot of each other,' he said quietly, 'and we're getting off to a bad start. I thought it might help us to get to know each other before we get off on some irrational, premature hate routine that will hurt everyone in this family.'

Faye couldn't think of a thing to say, especially because she saw in his clear blue eyes not a spark of laughter now. He was dead serious. Remorse overwhelmed her. This man was her brother's friend, Uncle Kai to the children who loved and admired him. She had been positively hateful and she knew it wasn't in her nature to be that way. She wasn't herself. She'd done the same thing to her parents and brother, who had tolerated her bad temper with patience and sympathy. She hated the world and took her misery out on everybody who had the back luck to cross her path. They were not to blame for what had happened to her, but it seemed as if she wanted to punish people, hurt them as she was hurting herself. There was pain and anger inside her and she didn't know how to get rid of it.

She swallowed helplessly, clenching her hands into fists, and looked straight into the calm blue eyes.

'I owe you an apology,' she said quietly. 'My rude behaviour was uncalled-for. I'm not usually so bitchy.'

A slow smile warmed his face, his eyes. 'Apology accepted.'

'Thank you. And ... and if the invitation still stands, I would like to have dinner with you.'

'Good! And with your permission I'll call you Faye.'

'Oh! Yes, of course. You knew my name?'

'Have known it for a long time. *Auntie* Faye from Chicago, right?' He grinned, his eyes narrowing in laughter. 'I won't tell you what image I'd conjured up from that description.'

'I have an idea,' Faye answered, smiling at him, his eyes holding hers captive until finally she tore her gaze away.

'I'll get dressed,' she said a little breathlessly, and fled. Those eyes were getting to her.

He looked at her appreciatively when she came back a while later. He was sitting again, leafing through a *National Geographic* magazine, the empty glass where he had left it.

'Pink,' he said, 'very daring with hair like that.'

The soft wool dress with its loose cowl neck and gathered sleeves was a subtle, dusty shade of pink and it looked nice, red hair or no. A true pink would have been anybody's nightmare.

'Don't tell me you expected green,' said Faye, and he shook his head.

'An original like you would come up with something else, I knew that. You look gorgeous, but starving. Let's go.' From beside his chair he picked up a Stetson and positioned it on his head, then leaped up and helped her into her coat before he picked up his own from a chair. It was a short sheepskin affair with thick wool curling around the edges. He looked magnificent, Faye had to admit. With that wide-brimmed hat and those leather boots he had Texas written all over him, without even having to open his mouth.

His car was not what she expected. It wasn't a pick-up truck, a flashy Mercedes, or a racy sports car, any of which would have suited him, one way or the other. Instead he led her to a Volkswagen Rabbit.

'What's the matter?' he asked. 'Don't you like

VW's?' Apparently he had noticed her surprise, although it was quite dark outside by now and he couldn't have deciphered much of her facial expression. Unless, of course, he was used to people's reactions to his car.

'It's not that,' she said, taken aback a little. 'It's just that. . . .'

'. . . it's out of character. You'd expected me to be driving something quite different, right?' He had eased himself behind the wheel, switched on the inside light and looked at her face, his expression faintly amused.

Faye shrugged lightly. 'Well . . . yes, I guess so.'

'Let me tell you something, little Faye,' he drawled, 'I'm probably not very much like anything you might imagine me to be, so don't make up your mind too fast.' He paused. 'And don't characterise me, put a label on me. Please.'

'You're one of a kind, an original,' she commented, and knew instinctively that it was so, even though she didn't know him very well as yet.

'Ask my father,' he said drily, switching off the inside light and starting the engine. 'I'll tell you about Texas some time, and about Texans, and you'll find I'm not exactly a stereotype.'

They drove through long, curving avenues, tree-lined and with houses set back from the road amid tall, dark evergreens.

'Any particular preference?' Kai asked. 'We have any imaginable kind of restaurant in this area. Japanese, Indian, Lebanese, Mexican—you name it.'

Faye hesitated. 'I hate to say this, but what I'd really like. . . .'

'. . . is a steak and a baked potato and salad.'

He seemed to be in the habit of finishing sentences for her, and again he was right. She didn't feel like eating anything very exotic, but she was hungry.

'No imagination, I know,' she said apologetically.

'Hey,' he said softly, 'I don't expect dazzling creativity in every single thing you say or do. A steak it is. I know a good place in Westport.'

'Where do you live? Here in New Canaan too?'

He nodded. 'A few minutes from Chuck's house. I have a little stone cottage. Nothing like Chuck's place.'

Chuck's house was a beautiful white Colonial clapboard with black shutters on a sprawling, sloping lawn full of tall regal evergreens. Chuck and Anne had inherited the place from Anne's grandparents, and it was the reason Chuck now lived in this elite, aristocratic community.

'How did you ever end up here?' Faye asked. 'I mean, you're from Texas and most of your work as a consultant originates in Washington and New York, I imagine.'

He shrugged. 'Coincidence, really. Chuck and I did a lot of work together, and then we co-authored a book. I came here temporarily, and just stayed on. I like it here.' He smiled. 'I lived in Washington for years and I got tired of the atmosphere there.'

The restaurant had an atmosphere of quiet, elegant comfort and it wasn't busy on this Wednesday night. They were seated at a corner table and ordered drinks.

'I don't even know,' Faye said, 'what you were doing in the house—I mean, why you came.'

He was leaning back in his chair, tipping it a little. 'I got back from Nigeria late last night, and I came by the office this afternoon to see if there was any mail. I saw Chuck's car, but didn't find him in the house, so I knew he'd probably just walked over to his in-laws with the kids. Then I heard the shower running and I decided to wait, have a drink, and see what developed.' He paused, and his eyes held hers with their magnetic blue brightness. 'And see what I found.'

'A scrawny alley cat,' she said drily, and he threw back his head and laughed out loud. Then, when he started speaking, she silenced him with a quick gesture.

'Don't say anything. I apologised for my cattiness. My scrawniness I'm going to take care of starting tonight. I'll have cheesecake for dessert, and an Irish coffee to top it all off.'

'A hospital isn't the place to get fat,' he observed calmly, smiling a little.

Being Chuck's friend and close to his family he was probably aware of the things that concerned them and it wasn't surprising that he should know about her accident. Still, it seemed strange to Faye that a man she had met only a couple of hours ago should know so much about her.

'I was fed intravenously for a long time,' she told him. 'And after I got better, I ... I had another setback that didn't do my appetite any good.' She congratulated herself on her calm and rational statement of facts, but a strange nervousness settled in her stomach.

Kai took a drink, put the glass back on the table and looked at her closely. 'Chuck said you'd be here for a while, find a job in the city maybe. What about your fiancé? Isn't he in Chicago?'

Avoiding his eyes, she looked down into her glass. 'I'm not engaged any more,' she said tonelessly.

'I see.'

No, you don't, Faye retorted silently. You don't see at all.

'Does it hurt very much?' he asked after a silence, and his tone was so gentle that it made her look up again and see his face with its expression of concern and it surprised her a little.

She thought about his question, seeing Greg's face

in her mind's eye, remembering his look of total incredulity when she had broken off their engagement.

'No,' she said slowly, speaking more to herself than to Kai. 'I never really loved him.'

CHAPTER TWO

GREG had not rejected her when she had told him of her visit to Doctor Martin's office. He took the news the way she had expected him to take it—calmly, unemotionally. He took her in his arms and told her it made no difference.

Oh, but it does, she thought, it does!

He smiled at her reassuringly. 'You know what I want.'

Faye did. She knew exactly what he wanted, and having children wasn't part of it. Changing diapers wasn't his game, he'd rather play golf. He wanted to travel, enjoy himself, live a life without domestic hassles and retire early. Children demanded too much effort and attention; they were noisy, expensive, and an evil that could be prevented in these enlightened days, thank the Lord.

Greg kissed her, then held her away from him a little and once more smiled reassuringly. 'You're not short-changing me, honey. You know I never wanted children. Don't worry about me.'

She wasn't worried about him. She was worried about herself, her deepening sense of depression, the feeling that she was losing control over her own destiny. She had lost a sense of direction, a sense of purpose. Somewhere in her life there was a big hole, a black emptiness. She wanted to be a mother, have babies, care for them and watch them grow. She had always wanted that, and she had thought lightheartedly that Greg would change his mind once they had been married for a while.

'I'm not worried,' she said flatly, and moved out of

his arms. 'I know you don't really care,' she added tonelessly.

Greg came to stand behind her, hands on her shoulders.

'I know you must be upset,' he said in a calm, detached sort of tone.

Upset? she thought hysterically. *Devastated* was a word closer to the truth.

And suddenly she saw him clearly—this man she was going to marry. Greg did not understand. And he never would, because it didn't touch his world. He wasn't open to sharing with her her innermost feelings of grief and anger. He was not capable of giving her understanding and support on any meaningful level, because all he really was concerned with was his own desires.

Shortly after that she had given him back his ring. He had not understood, but with some difficulty he had accepted the inevitable, for nothing could change Faye's mind.

She found herself staring at the candle in the middle of the restaurant table, and when she looked up her eyes met Kai's.

It was all over—Greg, Chicago, the accident. Now she was here in Connecticut, having dinner with a man she had met practically on arrival. He was watching her with a kind of gentle scrutiny, an interest, a real interest.

'You didn't love him, but you're hurt,' he said quietly. 'I can see it in your eyes.'

A slow warmth crept into her cheeks, and she shook her head. 'No. It's not . . . not the way you think.' She swallowed, looked away and her eyes caught the waitress bringing their food. She was relieved. She didn't want to continue this discussion.

The steak was good, cooked just the way she liked it. She scooped a generous amount of sour cream on her baked potato—the more calories the better. Ten, fifteen pounds and she'd look alive again.

'There's nothing wrong with your appetite now, is there?' Kai asked, his eyes amused as he watched her eat. 'Any particular after-effects of all that surgery you had? You can eat anything?'

'Yes,' she said with a sudden nervous fluttering of her heart. 'I was declared sound and solid, and I'll probably live to be a healthy hundred, or so one of my doctors said.' Only I'll never be able to have children, she added in silent thought. Small detail. Wasn't mentioned until much later.

Oh, stop the cynicism! she thought angrily, and took another bite of steak. Change the subject, talk about something else besides your medical misfortunes.

'Tell me about your work,' she said. 'You're still consulting, aren't you?'

Chuck and Kai had worked together as consultants before Anne died two years ago. For the welfare of his family Chuck had to give it up because it took him away for weeks at a time. Now he was teaching at the University, a job that afforded him time at home with his children. Still the two men shared the same office—part of Chuck's house designated for the purposes.

'Yes, I'm *still* consulting. You know about us consultants.' His voice was faintly mocking, for reasons Faye didn't understand.

'What do you mean by that?'

'There's a saying—If you can't do, teach. If you can't teach, consult.'

He didn't look like much of a loser to Faye. She had a hunch he would be successful at anything he tried. 'That's a generalisation, a stereotype,' she said. 'I'm sure you don't fit it.'

'Thank you, ma'am,' he drawled, and smiled.

'Anyway, I intend to *do* again after a few years. Settle down with a wife and raise kids and crops.'

'I see,' she said tonelessly. 'In Texas?'

'Yes. I've seen a lot of the world, but I still can't see myself settling any place else. I grew up on a cattle ranch in the West—dry desert, dusty, desolate and beautiful. And I'm going back there and get myself a spread and turn it into Paradise.'

'Irrigation?'

He grinned. 'Right.'

'Make Paradise out of the desert,' she quoted with a smile.

'Right.' He grinned a crooked grin. 'I reckon it's rather a romantic way of looking at it. It's back-breaking work and crops can fail for any number of reasons.'

Faye enjoyed listening to him, the slow, easy tone of his voice inducing in her a sense of familiarity, as if he was someone she'd known for a long time, and felt comfortable with.

'Tell me about your job,' Kai asked after their Irish coffee had been served. 'What exactly did you do in Chicago?'

'I'm a translator, interpreter at times, writer. I worked for an international corporation.'

'What language?'

'French and Spanish both.'

'Not bad,' he said, looking at her appreciatively. 'What about the writing? Is that a sideline? Romantic stories to compensate for the hard tough business you deal with every day?'

She gave him a withering look which made him laugh.

'I'm a technical writer. I take business reports, market evaluations, recommendations, the kind of stuff you write, I imagine, and made decent English out of them.'

'Do I detect a note of scorn?' he drawled, one eyebrow lifted.

Faye shrugged. 'There are a lot of big shots in a lot of high places who couldn't write a passable paragraph to save their lives. No wonder there are so many conflicts and arguments—nobody understands what the other is trying to get across.'

'If you're looking for a job,' he said, a grin spreading across his face, 'Washington, D.C. is the place for you.'

'Or the U.N., in New York,' she said cockily.

Full of humour, his eyes held hers. 'What I like,' he said slowly, 'is a woman with confidence and ambition.'

Confidence and ambition. Those were the operative words for her future. She would have to build a career—a career that would be meaningful and give her a sense of fulfilment.

The conversation went on, covering politics, Women's Liberation, music.

'I used to play in one of those honkytonk bands when I was a kid,' Kai told her. 'Played at country dances on Saturday nights.'

Faye was intrigued. This man was full of surprises. He travelled all over the world, and worked in many countries, gathering sophisticated and cosmopolitan ways. Still, here he was in leather boots and large-brimmed hat talking about playing in a honkytonk band. She tried to visualise him as a sixteen-year-old boy, but couldn't.

'What did you play?' she asked.

'Guitar. And I sang too. I even wrote some songs.' Apparently it was an amusing memory, gathering from the expression on his face and the glitter of humour in his eyes.

'You wrote songs? Really? Do you remember them?'

'Let me see.' He frowned, trying to remember, his lips twitching a little. 'Something like this: *Surrender, surrender, to my love sweet and tender. I'll love you for ever, even though you're not clever.*'

Faye groaned as if in pain. 'I'm sorry I asked. I get the picture. Don't tell me you put that stuff to music and sang it.'

'Sure I did. Had a lot of success with it too,' he drawled. 'Maybe some day I'll even sing for you.'

It had been weeks since Faye had felt as light-hearted as she did now, weeks since she'd felt free and easy laughter bubbling inside her. The company of this man was like a miracle potion. A great cure for anger and pain, or at least relief from it.

The meal finished, Kai paid the bill and stood up. With a sweeping gesture he covered his head with his Stetson, while several pairs of curious eyes watched him. It was hard to miss him, Faye decided. His tall muscular physique was difficult to ignore and seemed to dwarf everybody around him.

It was cold outside and Faye shivered. Kai's hand rested lightly on her shoulder as he guided her to the car and although it was nothing but a casual gesture, it seemed to her strangely intimate to feel the pressure of his hand on her body.

They were back in New Canaan when Kai pulled off the road into a secluded spot and stopped the engine.

Here it comes now, Faye thought with unaccountable disappointment. High school routine, no class at all. Park the car in a lovers' lane and kiss the girl.

He didn't.

'Well,' he said, 'what do you think? Did the meal establish a peaceful relationship between the favourite aunt and the favourite uncle?'

For a moment she was taken aback, then she laughed. 'So far so good. You really care about Darci and Joey, don't you?'

'Yes, I do. They're good kids, but I didn't stop here to talk about them. We need to make a decision.'

Faye didn't trust the glitter in his eyes. It promised nothing good.

'What decision?'

He motioned to the road. 'Left or right?'

'Left or right? What do I know. . . .'

'Your place or mine.'

'Mine!' Her reaction was immediate and forceful and Kai burst out into thunderous laughter.

'Nice and safe with Chuck and the kids at home?'

She smiled sweetly. 'You've got it.'

'Well,' he said, sighing gravely, 'that's that.' But the laughter was still in his eyes as he started the engine and drove on.

They entered the living room through the office, for which Kai had a key, but although several lights were on, nobody was there. Faye found the children asleep in their beds, and a light was on in Chuck's bedroom. It wasn't late yet, but she knew he liked to read before he went to sleep. She went back to the living room, but saw no Kai. He was in the kitchen making coffee. He was at home in this house, no doubt about that.

He put the mugs on the coffee table and took Faye's hand, pulling her down on the couch next to him. Then, before she had any way of doing anything about it, he was kissing her. It was a firm, confident kiss, as if he hadn't a doubt in the world that she would accept it.

And she did. She felt no offence and no rebellion, only a slight, faint wariness. *Don't lose your head. Keep it light and easy.*

Still, an unexpected quiver ran through her, a sensual stirring of her blood.

When he looked up, only a moment later, his eyes were smiling. 'You're very nice,' he said in his slow, easy tone. 'I'm enjoying your company.'

'I'm having a good time too,' she said lightly. 'And the coffee is getting cold.'

He didn't move, preventing her from leaning over and getting her cup. 'I don't care,' he said softly. His hands moved up and touched her hair. 'I like your hair, nice and thick and curly. Feels good.' His eyes moved over her face. 'There's a kind of sweetness about you. You're pretty. You're funny. You're nice.'

'There's one thing I'm not,' she said, smiling up at him.

He raised his brows in question. 'Oh?'

'Willing.'

'Mmm. Why not? Don't you like me?'

'You're a wolf.'

He grinned. 'And you're Little Red Ridin' Hood? Only I don't eat innocent little girls. I treat them more gently.'

'I can imagine. You devour them with charm.'

Kai shook his head disapprovingly. 'You've got it all wrong. I don't know what gives you ideas like that,' he drawled. 'Sure you don't want to come home with me? It's still early. I've got some nice wine and some good records and. . . .'

'. . . some interesting etchings on your wall?' she finished for him. 'Are you planning to seduce me?'

He looked at her, feigning shock. 'Now whatever gave you that idea?'

'I know all about wolves like you, besides. . . .'

'Yes?'

'My mother warned me. She said I should never go to bed with a man the first time I met him.'

'No? Why not? It could be very nice.' His eyes were full of blue sparks.

'She said it would be too embarrassing if I woke up the next morning and couldn't remember his name.'

He laughed so hard, it loosened his grip, an opportunity she took advantage of to disentangle herself and scoot over to the end of the couch. Quickly Faye picked up the cup from the table, leaned back comfortably, and began to drink her coffee.

The next morning Kai arrived at the office early, to make sure he'd see the children before they went to school.

Little Darci, dark hair flying, threw herself in his arms and got buried in his embrace. Joey confiscated the Stetson and with hands on imaginary guns, proceeded to do a John Wayne routine, shooting make-believe bad guys all over the living room.

'I bought you a present,' Darci said importantly. 'I'll go get it.'

It was a tie, a monstrosity in both colour and design. Kai admired it with great sincerity. 'This,' he said gravely, 'is a very special tie.'

'I picked it out myself,' Darci told him, dark eyes shining. 'You don't wear ties much, like Daddy, so I thought maybe you needed one. I wanted it to be nice for you, with lots of colours. You like colours, don't you?'

'Absolutely. Especially orange and pink.' Over Darci's head, Kai winked at Faye. 'I'll wear a shirt tomorrow and put it on and then when you come home from school you can tell me how it looks.' He kissed Darci on the cheek. 'Thank you, Pickle.'

Pickle. He calls her Pickle, Faye thought in amused surprise. Leave it to a man like Kai to come up with a nickname like that!

True to his word, Kai arrived the next day wearing the tie, the white of his shirt doing nothing to subdue the gaudy colours. Chuck and the children had already left for work and school and Faye was the only one at home to greet him.

She maintained a meaningful silence and gave him a

long, penetrating look. Kai returned the stare, taunting her.

'Words fail me,' she said at last.

'This is a very special tie,' he said slowly, eyes laughing. 'Not every man gets a tie like this.'

'I know what you mean. I hope you'll keep it for special occasions only.'

'Definitely. *Very* special occasions—like going out to dinner with you. How about Saturday night?'

Faye hesitated. 'You just took me out two nights ago.'

'Who's counting? I enjoy your company and I'd like to get to know you better.' The blue eyes looked at her intensely, seducing her into compliance.

Faye succumbed. 'Okay, I'd love to.'

He smiled winningly. 'Good!' He pointed to the door leading to the office. 'I'm going to be in there all day, working on my Nigeria report. It's going to be a hell of a job and. . . .'

'. . . you don't want to be disturbed.'

He grinned. 'Wrong. I like interruptions. Just come in and say hello,' he said gravely, 'or join me for a cup of coffee.'

Nothing wrong with that, was there? So she brought him coffee and they talked—about his work, and hers. About Texas, about the children, until she would leave him to get back to his work, feeling guilty for taking his time.

Dinner on Saturday was more of the same—easy talk and easy laughter with a hint of something else hanging in the air between them, a sense of waiting, a kind of awareness. They went to a night club for an after-dinner drink and listened to a jazz band, musicians who were enjoying themselves making up their music as they went along.

'So it's not only honkytonk music you like?' Faye

asked, and Kai shook his head, smiling disapprovingly.

'Are you still working on the stereotype, little Faye? You're in for a few surprises.'

'I like surprises.'

His smile deepened. 'Good. I have a lot in store for you.' He paused, holding her gaze. 'Your place or mine?'

She gave him a long, silent look.

'You don't give up easily, do you?' she asked at last.

He grinned. 'Do I look like a man who says: "When at first you don't succeed, give up"?'

Faye shook her head slowly. 'No. Do you always get what you want?'

Laughter glimmered in his eyes. 'Always,' he said softly. It sounded like a promise, and in the back of her mind a warning light flashed briefly.

He took her home without any further argument, let both of them into the house and caught her face between his hands. He looked deep into her eyes and Faye was overwhelmed with a sudden, peculiar sense of weightlessness—as if she were floating . . . drowning. Drowning in that bright blueness of his eyes that reminded her of vast clear skies and still blue lakes.

'I like you, Faye,' he said softly. 'I like you very much.'

'I like you too,' she whispered, and it was true, and there was a need to admit it. She closed her eyes and he kissed her then and she knew that all evening she'd been waiting for it. His kiss was soft and gentle and he let her go much too soon. Her eagerness seemed strange to herself, and his restraint surprised her. Somehow it should have been the other way around. Certainly he wasn't giving up on his seduction campaign yet!

He was watching her with a kind of amused speculation and for a brief moment there was silence. Then a faint smile curved his lips.

'I'm not a wolf,' he said quietly, touching her cheek very gently. 'Goodnight, Faye.'

As she watched the red lights of his car disappear down the drive, she wondered what exactly he had meant.

Start New Life. It was the item on top of her list, sub-divided in other categories—*Buy New Clothes*, *Find New Job.*

Find New Man? No. She wasn't ready for a long-term serious involvement. First she needed to sort out her feelings—her feelings about herself, her identity as a woman. Maybe it would take a long time before she was at ease with the new knowledge about herself. Before she could accept herself as she was without that miserable sense of inadequacy that overwhelmed her every time she thought about it. She had to find her-self before she could give herself to any man.

First she would have to find a job, try to make a career for herself.

'Take your time,' said Chuck when she asked him for advice. 'Wait for the job you really want. There's no hurry.' He smiled. 'We like having you here. It's nice for the kids, too.' There was warmth in his eyes and Faye was touched. Chuck was not a man of many words, one who expressed himself easily.

She made friends with Mrs Brown, the house-keeper, a short, round woman in her fifties. She was friendly, talkative, and the children loved her. She arrived in the morning at ten, made coffee for Kai if he was in his office, then set to work with efficient speed, loading washer and dryer, and unloading the dishwasher that Chuck had filled and switched on before he left. She dusted and vacuumed when necessary and went grocery shopping once a week. When the children came home from school at three she was ready with a snack and had a cup of tea herself while she listened to their stories. By five or six Chuck would come home, find dinner ready, and Mrs Brown would leave. It was an ideal arrangement, and Faye knew Chuck had been lucky to find a warm and caring person like Mrs Brown to be home with the children after school.

Kai was in the office every day for the next week, working on an article he was writing for an international publication. Faye would go in to see him a couple of times each day, have coffee with him, or share a sandwich lunch.

'You'd better watch out,' Mrs Brown said one day. 'He's a ladies' man, and he loves 'em and leaves 'em. Don't misunderstand,' she added hastily, afraid she had said too much, 'he's a nice man, too nice for his own good. The women fall all over him. Just don't get yourself hurt, is all I mean.'

Faye laughed. 'Don't worry, I won't.'

Mrs Brown looked doubtful. 'He's very handsome, and those eyes . . . I never seen such blue eyes!'

Neither had Faye. It was Kai's eyes that held her spellbound sometimes, that made her heart flutter crazily when he looked at her with that sparkle of laughter in them. A charmer, a real charmer was Kai Ellington.

One morning when they were having coffee, Kai gave her some sheets of paper. 'Here, what do you think of this?'

It was a report on an agricultural project in Guatemala. Faye read the papers with growing alarm. Was this Kai's report? Never before had she seen writing like that, and she'd thought she'd seen the worst.

'Is this yours?' she asked.

'What's the matter? Don't you like it?'

She took a deep breath. 'The writing is terrible! I can't judge the content, but then neither can anyone else, because it's buried in drivel.' Her eyes scanned the paragraphs. No way was this writing his—it couldn't be.

Faye put the paper down on his desk. 'This jewel of eloquence isn't yours, is it?' If it was she'd probably made an enemy for life.

He shook his head. 'No. I came across it this morning and I thought you might enjoy it.'

'How about showing me something that *is* yours?'

'All right, here.' He handed her a folder, and she realised it was the article he had been working on. She read a few pages, aware of him watching her.

'Not bad,' she said calmly.

His eyes narrowed. 'Meaning you could do better?'

'Of course—that's my profession. And I'm good.'

'Modest too,' he added dryly.

Faye shrugged. 'Look here, for example. Turn these two paragraphs around. And this sentence you can scratch, it's redundant.'

'How about you doing it? Rewrite and edit the whole thing, and I'll pay you.'

Had she heard right? She wasn't sure what reaction she had expected, something intimidating maybe, something that was supposed to cut her down to size.

'Really?'

'Sure. It's an important issue, and a well-written article may get it the attention it deserves.'

She smiled at him. 'Actually,' she said slowly, 'I hadn't expected you to take that kind of criticism from a mere woman.'

Kai's eyebrows rose in question. 'Why not? You're the expert. I imagine your French is a lot better than mine too.' He grinned, provocation in the blue eyes. 'I may be wonderful, but I'm not perfect.'

'Not modest, either.'

'That makes two of us, then.'

Faye grimaced and laughed. 'When do you want to have it finished?'

'Take your time, there's no hurry.'

Faye outdid herself. The finished article was a totally professional job—precise and concise till the very last comma. On Wednesday morning she went to Kai's office and handed it to him, feeling ridiculously nervous. It hadn't exactly been the greatest challenge she had ever encountered professionally, so why did she feel that way?

She watched him while he read it, his eyes quickly moving along the lines. He was pleased, very pleased, she could tell. When he was finished, he looked up and smiled.

'There's power in a well chosen word, isn't there? You injected a lot of power with some expertly chosen words.'

'Thank you,' she said, feeling absurdly pleased by his recognition.

She refused payment. There was no way she was going to accept money from him. She'd regarded the job more as a way to prove herself than as a way to make money. But Kai seemed quite surprised at her refusal.

'This is business,' he said. 'You worked on this job for a long time and you should be paid for your efforts.'

Faye shook her head. 'I would like you to accept it as a gesture . . . a token of. . . .' Her voice trailed away. His eyes held hers locked and it seemed impossible to speak.

'Yes?' he said softly, holding her gaze. The room was filled with a sense of expectation, as if the words she was about to say were of great importance.

'As a token of friendship,' she said.

CHAPTER THREE

THERE was a short silence, giving her words added significance.

'Thank you, Faye,' Kai said slowly, and the smile in his eyes made a warmth spread through her body and an uneasiness filled her. He stood up and came towards her, reached out and took her hand. His eyes kept holding hers and she couldn't move to save her life. She felt hypnotised by the brilliance of those blue eyes, so bright in the dark face.

'You're trembling,' he said softly.

'Fatigue,' she murmured. 'My kind of brilliant writing takes a lot of energy.'

'Of course,' he said, as if he took her seriously. His eyes moved down to her lips. 'And I'd like to thank you properly.'

With her heart thudding, Faye watched his face moving closer, felt his lips as they closed over hers and a sweet thrill of excitement quivered down her spine. There was the helpless knowledge that she couldn't play it cool, not with a man like Kai. His charm was potent like warm wine, its effect inevitable. His arms held her lightly against him, his lips moving gently over hers, teasing her into response. Then his arms tightened around her and the touch of his lips grew firmer, his kiss more intimate. Faye abandoned all reserve—she couldn't do anything else, didn't *want* to do anything else. For a few elusive moments they were swept off into some lovely world of sensuous delight, a place full of wonder and sweet excitement. She held him and kissed him and touched him without restraint because it was good and natural and the only way she was capable of responding.

When finally they withdrew, she felt lightheaded, off balance, aware of a faint embarrassment at her own lack of restraint.

'This is neither the time nor the place to get carried away,' he said, his voice low and a little husky. He was smiling, but there was an unfamiliar darkness in the blue eyes.

'I didn't mean that as a come-on,' she said, her voice faint. 'I was talking about friendship.'

His smile deepened and he touched her cheek, briefly. 'I don't know of a more promising beginning.'

'I think I'd better let you get back to work,' she said unsteadily, moving towards the door. She opened it and fled.

She almost ran to her room. The wolf, she thought, the wolf is at my heels. She sat down on the bed and let out a deep sigh, then gave a soft laugh. She couldn't even get mad at him. He was the nicest man she'd ever met. Also the most handsome, the most exciting, the most charming.

I don't have a chance, she thought with resignation, but somehow the thought did not alarm her. Was there any harm in having a little lighthearted romance with Kai? To play along with him? Love 'em and leave 'em was his game, according to Mrs Brown, and two could play at that.

Chuck woke her from troubled sleep two nights later. She had been crying again, huddled into a tight ball under the covers, and she gasped for air as she sat up. No memory of dreams, only a deep nameless ache. Always that same pain following her day and night, intensifying in her sleep when conscious thought could not subdue it.

Chuck was sitting at the edge of her bed, watching her intently. 'Tell me about it,' he said.

She shook her head, feeling dazed. 'I don't remember. There's nothing—no dream, just this feeling. . . .' Her voice trembled, faded away.

'What feeling?' he asked.

She swallowed. 'That I'm all alone.' Her voice was toneless. 'That there's nothing, nobody, and I'm . . . I'm. . . .' New tears brimmed over and she clenched her hands into fists, but she was powerless to suppress the sobs that overwhelmed her again, racking her body. Chuck took her in his arms, stroking her hair as if she were a child.

'Faye,' he said after she had calmed down, 'what happened between you and Greg?'

'It isn't Greg,' she said. 'I broke off our engagement myself. Greg and I . . . we're different. I never really loved him.'

He was silent. Did he believe her? Faye took a deep breath, blew her nose unelegantly.

'I'm sorry I woke you up. I'm all right now, really.'

Chuck gave her a long, searching look. 'Remember, you're not alone, Faye,' he said slowly. 'You have a family and we all love you. We care about you.'

'I know.' She reached for his hand. 'Thank you.' Her voice trembled. 'I love you too.'

'When you want to talk about it, I'll be here. That's what big brothers are for, remember?'

She remembered. He'd always been there when she needed him. Eight years older than she, he had been a hero in her eyes—big, strong, ever ready to come to her rescue. He had helped her with her homework, taught her how to roller-skate, listened to her when she had boy trouble and needed to talk. And now here he was again, ready to listen, and she couldn't tell him. It was locked inside her like some terrible secret she couldn't reveal.

She looked at him and swallowed, feeling miserable. 'Thank you.' She moved away from him and pulled the covers up. 'I'm all right now,' she said, managing a weak smile.

Chuck stood up, looking down at her with worry in his eyes. 'Good night, Faye. I hope you sleep well.'

She watched him go, feeling disloyal, distrustful. Why couldn't she have told him? Why was it so hard to let it out? She buried her face in the pillow, her whole body tense with the effort not to break out in tears again.

Why me? The angry question kept repeating itself, finding no answer. *Why me? Why me?* The words echoed in her mind all through a restless, troubled sleep.

The children's noisy laughter woke her in the morning and for a while she lay still, watching the sunlight filtering through the curtains. It looked like a beautiful day. With a sigh she finally swung her legs over the side of the bed and stood up.

She pushed the curtains aside and opened the windows and soft, balmy spring air softly touched her face. Spring. It was her favourite season, only this year she found little joy in the new life that erupted everywhere around her. It seemed to remind her only of her own inability ever to produce new life.

Produce new life. It sounded so dramatic and so overly romantic, and Faye certainly had never thought in that way about having children. Not until now.

She shook her head impatiently and pushed back a curl from her forehead. With a sigh she turned away from the window. She felt tired, a kind of dull weariness making her mind and body feel heavy. Then, suddenly angry with herself, she quickly dressed and went down for breakfast, trying hard to look cheerful.

It was later than usual when she heard Kai's car come up the driveway. The children had left for school long ago, and Chuck, too, had left, and Faye was drinking a second cup of coffee.

Kai gave a short rap on the living room door, then entered, as he did most mornings, and when Faye turned her head to greet him, words wouldn't come.

No Stetson, no boots. Instead he was dressed in a dark blue pin-striped suit, white shirt and dark tie. He looked stunning, there was no other word for it—handsome in a very conventional way, with the blond hair and blue eyes bright as ever, his tan standing out against the whiteness of his shirt.

She caught his amused look, and grinned. 'You look very ... er ... impressive,' she managed to say.

'Good. I'm going to Washington today to have one of those famous two-Martini lunches and drum up some more business.'

'I didn't know.' He hadn't mentioned he was going anywhere.

'Neither did I. I got a phone call at home last night. I'm here to get some papers and then I'll be on my way to La Guardia to catch a shuttle at eleven or so.'

The phone rang and Faye answered it, finding an agitated Mrs Brown on the line. The car wouldn't start, she said. A tow truck was coming to take it to the garage, and she'd have to wait for a taxi to bring her to the house and she had no idea how long that would take.

'Why don't you take the day off?' Faye suggested. 'I'm capable of managing on my own for a day. I'll be here when the kids come home from school, don't worry about it.'

'But Darci has a birthday party to go to!' Mrs Brown wailed. 'I was going to drive her over there. I don't know what to do!'

'The birthday party, right.' Faye remembered now and she frowned, trying to find a solution. She didn't have a car here; both the children's grandparents were working, so she couldn't appeal to them for help. Then her eyes caught sight of Kai, dangling his car keys in front of her.

'Take my car,' he said.

'Mrs Brown,' she said into the phone, 'hold on for a moment, please.' She looked at Kai, eyebrows raised. 'You need your car to get to the airport, don't you?'

He shrugged. 'I can take the limousine.' He looked at his watch. 'I imagine they'll have a seat for me at this hour, and I've plenty of time. You'll have to take me there, though.'

'Of course, yes. Thank you!'

'No problem.'

Faye returned to the phone. 'I have Kai's car, Mrs Brown. Everything's settled.'

Mrs Brown, relieved, insisted on coming to work just the same, so Faye arranged to pick her up at home after she had dropped Kai off at the limousine stop.

'Spring is beautiful here,' she said to Kai as they were driving along the winding lanes, past rustic stone walls and sweeping green lawns. 'Another week or so and the leaves will be out. The weather man is calling for rain tonight,' she added after a few moments' silence. 'By the looks of it you'd think the sun was going to shine for ever.'

'It's a rainstorm they're expecting, not just rain,' said Kai. 'I hope I make it back before it gets too bad.'

A thought stirred in the back of her mind and she shifted uncomfortably in her seat.

'Thank you for letting me have your car,' she said. 'Are you sure you trust me with it?'

One eyebrow quirked up. 'Shouldn't I?'

She shrugged. 'I don't know. A few months ago I was in an accident. My car was a write-off and so was I, just about,' she said flatly.

'The information I have,' he said slowly, 'is that a

man with too many drinks in him came racing around a bend on the wrong side of the road and crashed into you head-on. He killed himself, wrecked his own car, wrecked yours, and nearly killed you. I don't see how that casts a negative reflection on your driving.'

Faye looked down on her hands in her lap. 'I keep thinking,' she said tonelessly, 'that there must have been something I could have done to avoid him.'

'I can't imagine what. You couldn't even see him coming, and he was doing sixty in a residential area.' He looked at her searchingly. 'Are you still worried about it? Do you still think about it a lot?'

Faye shook her head. 'No, just sometimes.' There were other things on her mind now.

'Good.' He smiled. 'Anyway, as far as I'm concerned, you can have my car any time. Most of the time it's just sitting in the driveway anyway.'

'Thank you'. His generosity touched her, made her feel a little uneasy too.

They arrived at the limousine stop and Kai parked the car and switched off the engine. 'I'll probably be late coming home tonight,' he said. 'Eight or nine, something like that. Suppose I can charm you into picking me up here?' There was a teasing smile in his eyes and Faye wondered what he was thinking. She had his car, didn't she? Of course she'd pick him up. She smiled back at him, feeling a little reckless, suddenly.

'Try me,' she taunted.

He leaned forward, his face very close, his eyes glinting. 'I like you,' he said softly. 'You're beautiful. I love your freckles and your red hair and. . . .' He paused, his eyes on her mouth. 'I love those warm lips.' One finger softly touched her mouth, moved down her chin and slowly, seductively trailed down her throat as his eyes followed the movement. 'And your soft round. . . .'

Faye jerked upright, heart pounding. 'You've got it,' she said in a businesslike tone. 'I'll be there.'

He laughed, saying nothing, his eyes back on her face.

Faye didn't avert her eyes. 'You're irresistible, aren't you?' she said, smiling a little, because really, he was.

'So are you.'

'It's ten in the morning,' she said primly, wondering in silence how he would charm a girl into bed with the added advantage of the night-time atmosphere.

'I know,' he said, with mock apology in his voice. 'I'm better at night.'

'With the help of candlelight, wine and music?'

'Right. How about it?' It was an invitation, and she knew it, but before she could answer, he bent over and kissed her full on the lips. Then he straightened, lifted his briefcase off the back seat and got out of the car.

'See you tonight, Faye,' he said, a devilish gleam in his eyes. He closed the door and strode to the parked limousine. Faye slid over into the driver's seat and drove away. She caught his wave in the rearview mirror and she couldn't help grinning at nothing in particular. She felt very light and happy, suddenly, and very reckless.

It was after eight when he called from the airport, telling Faye the limousine was about to leave and could she pick him up in about an hour? Of course, she said, she'd be there.

'How's the weather?' he asked.

'Terrible. The weather report was right for once. It's raining and it's very windy.'

'Here, too. The plane could barely land. Well, I'll see you in an hour or so.' He rang off, and Faye went to the kitchen to put the dinner dishes into the dishwasher and make coffee for Chuck and herself.

Chuck had built a fire and he was sitting in front of it with Darci and Joey, reading them a story.

'Faye,' he said when she came back into the living room, 'why don't I go and get him? The weather is awful and it's dark, and you're not familiar with the roads.'

It made sense, didn't it? Only she didn't want Chuck to pick Kai up. She wanted to do it herself. She had counted on seeing him again, and she refused to analyse why she wanted to.

'I know the way,' she said lightly. 'You're tired, and I've hardly done anything at all today.'

Except help Mrs Brown clean out the refrigerator, make the beds, bake a cake, shop for groceries. But Chuck didn't know that.

'I'm not so tired I can't drive to the limousine stop,' he said reasonably.

'I'll do it, I don't mind,' Faye insisted, and he gave her a quizzical look, but dropped the subject.

The limousine arrived at the same time Faye did, and she watched Kai get out, the collar of his trench coat up. He made a dive for the car, got in behind the wheel, letting out a heavy sigh.

'This weather is downright depressing,' he said. 'And I'm starved.' He started out of the parking lot and gave Faye a quick glance. 'You've had dinner already, of course.'

'Yes.'

He sighed. 'Well, I'll go home and have a lonely dinner.' He paused significantly. 'Unless, of course, you'd come with me and keep me company. I'd like some company.'

'Sure,' she said. 'Why not?' And she was as surprised as he was at her answer. Or was she? She saw a slow grin spread across his features, and was aware of a slight but noticeable electricity in the air, a sense of excitement.

I'll probably live to regret this, she thought drily, but pushed the thought aside.

'Surprise, surprise,' Kai said softly, the devilish gleam back in his eyes.

'I come up with one now and then,' she said, smiling smugly, and he laughed out loud.

The driveway to his house was long and dark, and Faye couldn't see much of the surroundings, except tall, dark evergreens and a low rock wall separating the property from the road. Mostly everything looked wet and dark.

Kai entered the house ahead of her, switching on lights, and Faye looked around with delight. It was a small house, a cottage, really, furnished not in any particular style, but rather a mixture of different kinds of furniture that made up an interesting whole—cosy, warm, and with a distinct personal atmosphere.

There was a large, wheat-coloured contemporary couch and a worn leather chair that had probably lived through the last two world wars. An oriental rug lay on a dark polished floor and the walls were panelled with gleaming oak. One wall featured a large fireplace, and another was lined with shelves from floor to ceiling, full of books and stacks of magazines.

'I love this place,' Faye said, and meant it. 'It looks so. . . .'

'Lived in?' Kai supplied.

She smiled. 'Yes. For some reason I don't expect men to make much of their surroundings.'

'I spend half my life in hotel rooms. I don't need to come home to one.'

'Do you keep house yourself?' Faye asked.

'Somebody comes in once a week to give the place a good cleaning, for the rest I manage nicely on my own.' He produced a bottle of wine and poured both of them a glass. 'Now, if you'll excuse me for a minute, I'll get out of this suit and put on something a little more comfortable.' He began loosening his tie. 'Also, I'll give Chuck a call and tell him where you are.'

What was he going to tell him? Faye wondered as she stared at Kai's retreating back. *I've lured your sister home. Don't expect her back tonight?*

After he had eaten they went into the sitting room and Kai built a fire while she watched him from the couch.

A strange feeling was taking hold of her, a mingling of faint fear and exhilaration. She wasn't sure what she was expecting, what Kai had in mind now that she was here in his house, but she could make a few guesses.

Outside a full-fledged storm was now raging and she could hear the sounds of rain and wind above the crackling of the fire. A violent gust of wind rattled the window panes and somewhere in the distance a sudden crash overpowered all other noise.

'A tree,' Kai said levelly. 'In weather like this a few always go down.' He went over to the stereo, selected some records and put them on. Calm, quiet jazz, tuning out the noises from outside. Faye liked it. She snuggled closer into the corner of the couch, legs tucked beneath her, and Kai sat down in the old leather chair opposite her, stretching out his legs towards the fire.

'Are you warm enough?' he asked.

Faye nodded. 'Tell me about your day in Washington. How many Martinis at lunch?'

'Actually, I had only one. One drink in the middle of the day is quite sufficient for me.' He grinned. 'I like my brain clear when I'm working. I like to accomplish what I set out to accomplish.'

'Which you did, of course.'

'Of course.'

'What did you do after lunch?'

'I went to the State Department for two more meetings, which went very well, too, as expected.'

Confidence oozing out all over the place. He knew what he wanted and he got it.

'Tell me some more about Texas, your family, the ranch,' she invited.

He observed her with a lazy smile. 'I don't want to talk about that either.'

'What *do* you want to talk about?'

'You.' His eyes moved over her, slowly, suggestively. 'Have I told you before that you're beautiful?'

'No.'

But he had, at least a dozen times. He'd called her gorgeous, charming, lovable, bewitching, and a variety of other words even more outrageous.

He looked wounded. '*No?*'

'Well, maybe once or twice,' she relented, smiling sweetly.

He sighed. 'But it doesn't melt you down or soften you up, does it?'

She raised her eyebrows in mock surprise. 'Is that what you're trying to do—melt me down?'

Kai stretched out his legs more comfortably, smiled at her. 'Let's say I'm doing a preliminary investigation as to the viability of the project. If the potential outcome warrants the estimated inputs. . . .'

She threw a cushion at him, which he caught neatly.

'Don't you dare talk as if I'm one of your consulting projects!'

'Yes, ma'am,' he said meekly, but his eyes belied his quiet agreement. Suddenly, tossing away the cushion, he took one great leap towards her, pushed her down on the sofa and began to kiss her in an exaggerated imitation of the proverbial Latin lover.

The suddenness of his attack knocked her off guard and it took a minuté to register what was happening.

Then she moved her face away, gasping to catch her breath.

'What do you think you're doing!'

He had buried his face in her neck and she could feel slow laughter shake his body, but he didn't answer her.

She twisted beneath him, her heart thudding. 'I said what do you think you're doing?'

'I don't know,' he murmured against her skin. 'I just lost my mind.'

'You could've fooled me,' she said with mild sarcasm, pushing at his heavy bulk. 'Get off me!'

But he didn't. Instead he softly kissed her neck. 'Mmm,' he whispered. 'You smell good, you feel good. . . .' He looked up and when their eyes met suddenly everything changed. The joke was over. The laughter had gone from his eyes, and now all she saw was a deep, dark glowing that shook her to the very core. A sensuous warmth flowed through her—wonderful, frightening, exciting all at once. For a few timeless moments there was nothing but a quivering silence between them, their eyes locked in a wordless questioning and wondering.

'Faye. . . .' It was half a sigh, half a whisper. His lips came down on hers again and this time there was no teasing and no joking, only a deep, tender urgency that filled her with an unfamiliar hunger. Her arms went around him and she responded to his kisses, giving up caution and inhibition, because this was what she wanted, this was what she had been looking forward to all day.

An innocent little romance. There was no harm in that, was there? No harm in acknowledging that his charm was affecting her, that the blue eyes were speeding up her heartbeat, that she liked feeling his hard lean body against her.

But the way he was kissing her erased all further

thought from her mind, left no room for anything but the warm glow of excitement, and when he finally sat up, she was trembling.

He looked into her face, smiling. His fingers played with her curls, then slowly moved down her cheek and touched her lips. His eyes held hers as his hand trailed down her chin and throat. He didn't stop as he had done that morning, but continued till his hand covered her left breast, his eyes still on her face. Faye could feel warm colour surge into her cheeks as he gently caressed her, but in his eyes there was no teasing, only a tenderness that held no playfulness at all.

'Do you mind me touching you like this?' he asked softly, and she flushed deeper at his words. She couldn't move, couldn't avert her eyes, and she slowly shook her head, incapable of making a sound.

'I've wanted to do this ever since we met—touch you and hold you.' His hands moved up and took her face between them. 'You know what I'd like to do now, more than anything else? I'd like to take your clothes off, look at you, kiss you all over and make love to you.'

Her heart quickened. His words were like an intimate touch—sensuous, suggestive, and she couldn't stop herself from trembling. He had noticed it too, and he pulled her against him and for a while he just held her, very tightly, very quietly, then he let her go.

He stood up, pulling her into a sitting position.

'I'll get us a cup of coffee.'

Coffee. She couldn't believe it. Something was happening, but it wasn't in the script and it bewildered her. She heard water running and a minute later the gurgle and splutter of an electric drip coffee-maker. She got up from the couch, walked to the bookcase and examined the contents. When Kai came back into the room with the coffee she had herself under control again.

He sat down next to her on the couch, but not too close. 'Tell me about your ex-fiancé,' he said. 'What kind of man is he?'

His question took her by surprise. She swallowed, trying to think of something to say.

'He plays golf a lot,' she said at last, giving him a silly grin.

'Why did he break your engàgement?'

'He didn't.'

He observed her in silence, waiting.

'I . . . we weren't engaged very long. We weren't . . . weren't tuned in very well, emotionally, I mean.'

Faye couldn't think of any other way to describe it. A vague uneasiness, a feeling that something was wrong. She thought again of all the times Greg had asked her to marry him—and all the times she had said no. And then, in the hospital, when she was frightened and insecure and helpless she had finally given in. Greg had bought her a ring, a big sparkling solitaire diamond, and all the nurses had been envious. There had been a party in the hospital and the nurses and the doctors had all come in to congratulate her.

She lay in bed with the ring on her finger, looking at it, and it was too big and too conspicuous and it didn't feel right. It had never felt right.

'It was a mistake,' she said tonelessly.

'Are you over it?'

Faye nodded. 'I was relieved when it was over. I think I knew something was wrong all along.'

'I thought you went into a depression after your engagement broke up.'

Her coffee cup suddenly trembled in her hand and she stared numbly into the dark liquid. 'Chuck told you that?' Her voice was without inflection and she didn't look at him.

Kai's hand took her cup away and put it on the table. He lifted her chin and forced her to look at him.

'Faye, if it wasn't your engagement, then what did cause that depression?'

'Kai, I . . .' She swallowed miserably.

'Can't you tell me, please?'

'It was everything,' she said slowly. 'My whole life.' She was being evasive, and she knew it. 'A delayed reaction from my accident, I think. I had to make a change, put everything behind me and start over. That's why I'm here.' She paused, and he didn't answer. 'Why do you want to know?'

'It seems important.' There was a brief silence. Then he smiled and humour was back in his eyes. 'After all, a man wants to know that the woman in his arms isn't secretly pining for another man.' He was being evasive, too, she sensed it. He knew there was more to the issue than she was giving away.

'I'll set your heart at rest. I'm not pining for Greg, or anyone else, for that matter.' She met his gaze bravely. 'My mind and my body are in perfect harmony.' She was well aware of the provocation hidden in her statement. He didn't miss it, either—the devilish gleam in his eyes was proof of that.

'Hey, wait a minute,' he said softly, 'who is seducing whom?'

She looked at him innocently. 'Nobody is seducing anybody. But I do think I should go home. It's getting late.' She tried to stand up, but he pulled her down.

'Chicken,' he whispered in her ear, and his lips caressed her neck, moved up to her mouth, and she struggled helplessly for a few moments, then gave in. But when his kiss became more passionate, she tore away from him in sudden panic.

He laughed softly and his eyes were brilliant with blue sparks of humour and Faye knew he had been putting her on.

'I'm going home,' she said as calmly as she could.

'Scared?'

'No.'

'Liar.'

She didn't answer, but walked out of the room to find her coat, and Kai came after her and took it out of the hall closet and helped her into it. Pulling on his own, he opened the door and in silence they walked to the car, wind and rain assaulting them.

As they drove along the narrow, winding road, he began to talk about a contract he was about to sign for a three-week job in Nicaragua. He didn't seem disappointed or angry about her wish to go home. Maybe he had not really expected her to stay. Faye couldn't figure him out, and it confused her. Not that she was so sure about what she wanted herself.

A lighthearted little romance. But they were grown people and certainly Kai wasn't going to stay contented with kissing on the couch and flirting in the car. He wanted to make love to her—he had said that. And what about her? Did she want to?

It was an uneasy question, but she was too honest with herself to deny her true feelings. He was the most exciting man she had ever met, funny and a little crazy. And nice. His kisses and touches swept her away from reason and caution, giving her pure delight, and—yes, she wanted to make love.

Alarm overwhelmed her. How could she think such a thing? How could she consider sleeping with a man who didn't love her, have an affair without any serious commitment? It had never happened to her before— she'd never felt so captivated by a man's charm. In a strange way it frightened her.

They hadn't gone very far when Kai slowed the car down and brought it to a stop. Leaning forward, he peered through the wet windshield.

'Well,' he said levelly, 'guess what.'

Faye followed his gaze and through the pouring rain she noticed a tree blocking the road. It had broken off like a match somewhere near the bottom of the trunk, and she realised it must have been the crash they had heard earlier that evening.

'Now what?' she asked.

'A dream come true.' He grinned wickedly. 'Faye, girl, there's no escape. You'll have to spend the night with me.'

CHAPTER FOUR

'DON'T tell me there isn't another way out,' she said, apprehension creeping through her.

'There isn't,' he said calmly. 'This road dead ends not far past my house. I'll show you, if you don't believe me.'

'Never mind.' She looked at him warily. 'Are you sure you didn't order this from a disaster catalogue?'

He gave a hearty laugh. 'And delivered right on time, too.'

'You think this is funny, don't you?' she asked irritably.

'Yes, ma'am,' he drawled, exaggerating his accent, and Faye had a sudden wild urge to hit him. She was scared, and it made her mad. She didn't want to have to come to any decisions tonight. She had overplayed her hand. Kai turned the car and they drove back to his house and she couldn't think of a word to say. Inside once more, Kai made another phone call to Chuck to tell him what had happened.

'Do you suppose he believes you?' she asked, and he shrugged, smiling.

'Does it matter? You're a big girl, aren't you? Just as long as he knows you're not lying by the road some place.'

He turned, walked to the stereo and changed the records.

'Would you like to dance?' he asked, coming up to her and taking her hand.

Dance. Faye couldn't believe her ears. Couldn't believes her ears either when she heard the first slow movements of the music fill the room. Strauss. A *waltz*!

For a moment she was speechless. 'To this?' she managed at last.

He gave an amused laugh. 'Yes. I find Strauss eminently suitable for rainy days. Perks up the spirit, good for the soul.'

'I haven't waltzed since I was in dance school,' Faye said, still incredulous.

'You've missed something. Come on!' He swept her away and she had no choice but to follow his lead. He was superb, managing to avoid the furniture with flawless agility. It was like a dream, as if she wasn't touching ground at all, as if she were merely floating in his embrace. Images of girls in lacy, ruffled dresses came to mind, a ball at a royal court in historic times. And here she was, the most beautiful of all, floating in the prince's arms.

The waltz seemed to go on for ever, but finally it ended in a loud climax of sound. Faye stood in his arms, holding on dizzily. She leaned against him, trying hard to steady her breathing and her rapid heartbeat. After a few moments he held her away from him and studied her face, a half-smile curving his lips.

'If only you could see yourself,' he said slowly. 'Breathless, flushed and shiny-eyed.' He paused, his eyes on her face. 'And very kissable.'

Surprisingly, he didn't kiss her. Instead he led her to the couch saying he was going to get them something to drink. Faye was glad to be sitting. The record continued, filling the room with the lively sounds of a polka, and the atmosphere of romantic illusion persisted. Kai came back from the kitchen with two glasses and the bottle of wine he had opened earlier that evening.

'Can't say we're boozing it up,' he said. 'We can't even manage to finish a bottle between us.' He poured the wine and handed her a glass. 'A toast?' He clinked her glass, his eyes drawing hers. 'To us,' he said softly.

She could feel the colour creep into her cheeks and was annoyed by it. She was acting like a teenager out on her first date, intoxicated by the first sweet illusions of imagined love. But even Faye, twenty-three and not quite so green, was not immune to the amorous attentions of a handsome, virile man—the smiles and gentle kisses, the whispered words of love's desire.

He took her empty glass and put it on the table, then reached for her hand. 'The Blue Danube coming up. Shall we?'

Her initial reserve had fled altogether and fired on by the warmth of the wine spreading through her, she floated into his arms and once more drifted away in sweet fantasy, a fairy tale of love and riches and glamour. It was a sensuous pleasure to feel him guide her and swing her around as if she weighed nothing at all. She was aware of the muscled strength of his body, his total control over all his movements, and his nearness stirred in her a nervous exhilaration.

After the music had stopped he held her against him again for a few moments, and she was aware of a primitive yearning for him to stay close to her, not to break away, but at last he gently put her from him.

'No more lollygagging,' he said brusquely. Unexpectedly he swept her up in his arms and carried her from the room. 'Let's go to bed.'

There was no time to think. He pushed open a door, lowered her to the floor and after one swift glance Faye knew they weren't in his bedroom. It was a spare room, obviously so. From a closet he took sheets, blankets and a pillow and tossed them on to the single bed that was covered with a spread, but apparently not made up. Before she had quite recovered from this surprising change in events, Kai was making the bed and Faye moved automatically to help him. He was all business, suddenly, and it was hard to take. Was she disappointed? Relieved? She wasn't sure.

The bed finished, Kai straightened and threw her a calm smile. 'The bathroom is next door to the left. There are towels and whatever else you need. You want something to wear?' He turned for the door, not waiting for an answer. 'Wait, I'll be right back.' He returned a minute later and threw her a white T-shirt. 'Here, can't think of anything better. And I even happen to have an extra toothbrush.' He handed it to her. 'Compliments of Colgate. Came free with the tube I bought last week.'

'Thank you.' She made a helpless gesture with her hands. 'Kai, I . . . I'm confused.'

He smiled with warm amusement in his eyes. 'I know,' he said quietly. 'In more than one way.'

He was right, too. She didn't know what she wanted herself, what she should do. And his behaviour seemed out of character and added to her general bewilderment.

He came closer and lifted her chin. 'Let me clear up something, though,' he said slowly. 'My bedroom is straight across the hall. It has a bed big enough for two, and you have a standing invitation to share it with me . . . any time.'

She could feel herself grow warm, and then suddenly, out of nowhere her old bravado came back to her.

'Do I have to knock?' she asked demurely, and his laughter took away all remnants of discomfiture.

'No. Just come in and surprise me.' He dropped a kiss on her mouth. 'Goodnight, Faye.'

Something woke her from a deep sleep—a touch on her head, then her hand. She opened her eyes and closed them again against the bright light, but not before she had taken in Kai sitting on the edge of the bed, holding her hand.

'Are you planning to sleep all day?' He sounded amused and Faye came fully awake at the realisation of where she was. She struggled upright, opening her eyes as wide as possible in an effort to keep them from closing again.

'What time is it?'

'Nine-thirty.'

She stared at him in surprise. She hadn't slept late for ages. Not with Darci and Joey around the house, making noise that would wake bears out of hibernation. Faye sighed, extracting her hand from Kai's grip. 'I'll get up.'

'You don't have to. You look charming sitting there with my T-shirt on. I'll bring you breakfast in bed.'

'Not a chance.' The T-shirt was much too big, but there was no doubt that it housed a female figure, and she'd feel a whole lot more comfortable in her own clothes. Things looked different in the daylight—no wine to befuddle the senses, no Strauss to sweep away reality.

Kai laughed and stood up. He was already dressed, wearing black pants and a sweater the colour of his eyes. He stood in the sun streaming through the windows and he looked very tanned and very strong, like a tourist on a travel poster. He left the room, saying he was starting breakfast, and Faye got out of bed.

He was frying bacon and eggs when she entered the kitchen and the aroma made her suddenly ravenously hungry.

'Can I help?'

'No, thanks.' He turned and opened the refrigerator. 'What kind of juice would you like? There's a choice. I have orange, tomato, grapefruit and cranberry juice.'

He looked at her and she looked at him and she didn't immediately answer, her silence intentional.

'Quite a selection,' she said.

'Right.' His eyes were dancing. 'One never knows who might stay overnight.'

'Of course.'

'So, what will it be?'

Faye looked at him levelly, face expressionless. 'I'll have champagne, please.'

The silence that followed she had expected, but not the totally deadpan expression that appeared on his face.

'Of course,' he said slowly. 'Why didn't I think of that?' He strode out of the kitchen and Faye stared after him, dumbfounded. She hadn't meant for him to take her seriously. Champagne for breakfast. . . .

He returned with a bottle and she hastily came to her feet. 'Kai, please, don't open it! I was only joking!'

He grinned. 'Called your bluff, didn't I? Champagne it will be.' He began to open the bottle.

Faye sank back on her chair. 'Of course,' she said flatly, 'you happened to have champagne on hand. I should have guessed.'

'Always have a bottle around for special occasions. And this is a special occasion.'

'It is?'

His eyes were deep pools of laughter. 'I'd like to celebrate the fact that this is the first time we spent the night together.'

'You make it sound as if we'd shared the same bed!'

'I won't tell if you won't tell,' he drawled, grinning crookedly. And then with a plop the cork shot out of the bottle and the champagne started foaming out over the edge.

It was the most delicious breakfast Faye had ever eaten, and she wasn't sure whether it was due to Kai's company or the champagne, or the rather heady combination of both. She felt light and free, a sensation that she thought belonged to the past. But nothing mattered now but the present, the reality of this beautiful spring day, sunny, bright, matching her mood. Through the window she could see the sky, very blue, very clear—like Kai's eyes.

The storm had blown itself out to sea, vanished like the darkness of night, like her uneasiness and confusion. She looked at Kai across the table, saw the sun touching his thick blond hair, the strong brown hands holding his coffee cup, and a quietness came over her, a peacefulness she had never felt before. There was a knowing, a deep awareness that she would come to no harm from him. Kai Ellington played the game, but he played fair, leaving her to play by her own rules, at her own pace.

They stood up together and carried the dishes to the counter. She stood next to him, very close, and it seemed like the most natural thing in the world to turn towards him, put her ams around him and kiss him.

'Thank you,' she whispered.

His hands were warm on her back, his eyes smiling into hers, and he just looked at her, saying nothing, and he didn't have to. There was no need for words.

The week that followed Faye kept busy helping Mrs Brown, translating some Spanish material for Kai, and searching fruitlessly through the *New York Times* for a job. Her heart wasn't in it, she knew. She was enjoying the quiet relaxed life at home with Chuck and the children, away from pressures and demands and schedules that were part of the working life.

She enjoyed Kai's company, too. She spent time with him in his office, drinking coffee, talking, laughing. They went out for a meal, a movie, and everything between them seemed light and easy and no longer did she feel any apprehension when he kissed her and held her, and his seductive flirtations worried her no more. There was a right time for everything, and it would come, she knew. It was inevitable. She knew it and Kai knew it. It was only the fact that he didn't pressure her that surprised her.

They were in his office one morning when the phone rang. Kai, searching through a stack of papers, motioned to Faye to answer it and she lifted the receiver, offering a cheerful hello.

There was a momentary silence.

'Is this Kai Ellington's office?' A young female voice—light, pleasant, a little hesitant.

'Yes, it is.'

'May I speak to him, please? This is Judy Benton speaking.'

'One moment, please.' Faye handed Kai the receiver. 'Judy Benton,' she said, reaching for the door to leave.

He took her wrist, pulling her back, shook his head at her and talked into the phone all at once.

Faye didn't want to stay and listen to a personal phone call, if that was what it was, but she had no choice as he seemed determined to hold on to her. He was laughing at something Judy Benton said and a faint irritation welled up in her.

'What time?' Kai asked. 'Seven? Fine. I'll see you then.' He replaced the receiver, smiling at Faye.

'That,' he said calmly, 'was a woman.'

'I figured that,' Faye said equally calmly.

'A very beautiful woman.'

'I'm so pleased for you.'

His eyes held hers locked. 'Also, she's very married, very pregnant, and very fast with the typewriter.'

'Very interesting,' she said in a tone of voice that indicated that it was not.

'She works for me, typing final drafts of my reports. She works at home. I'm picking up some finished material tonight.'

Faye studied his face. 'Why are you telling me this?'

He was holding both her hands now and he pulled her closer a little and gave her a long, steady look.

'Because,' he said slowly, 'I want you to know.'

There was a silence and an uneasy thought faintly stirred in the back of her mind, then vanished.

'I wasn't terribly concerned,' she said lightly.

'I wouldn't want you to be.' His face came closer and she yielded to him and closed her eyes. His kiss was gentle, very gentle.

The days were growing longer and spring was there to stay. Dogwoods bloomed everywhere, a feast in white and sugary pink, and a veil of tender green adorned almost every tree and bush. In the grass by the side of the roads dandelions showed their yellow blooms, and the air was filled with the cheerful chirping of the birds.

Faye made concentrated efforts to enjoy her life of relative leisure, to banish disconcerting thoughts and painful memories, and to some degree she succeeded. In Kai's presence, it all seemed easier.

She had been gaining weight in the last few weeks and she was delighted. The hungry look was fading. Scrawny alley cat, she had called herself, and she laughed at the memory. Soon she would look like herself again, without all the bones sticking out, just smooth curves and soft shapes, nothing very spectacular, but nice enough.

Kai signed his contract and left for Nicaragua and Faye took him to Kennedy Airport. A strange feeling was taking hold of her, but she repressed it, refusing to acknowledge or analyse it. He was leaving for three weeks, hardly an eternity.

In the general noise and confusion of the departure lounge, they turned to each other to say goodbye, but no words would come when Faye looked at him, her tongue silent in her mouth. Then, wordlessly, he gathered her up into his arms and kissed her with such fierce passion, it staggered her. He left her standing, saying not a word of goodbye, and she stared after him, motionless.

Three weeks. It wasn't such a long time. Or was it? She tried not to think about it as she drove home.

The days went slowly and Faye's spirits began to sink lower and lower. She missed Kai; she missed him very much. The uneasy thought crossed her mind that maybe she was using her relationship with Kai as a crutch, or as a diversionary tactic to keep from dealing with the problem at hand—coming to terms with herself and her future. Was she depending on Kai to serve as a kind of anaesthetic for her emotional pain?

It seemed that her life was an up-and-down battle with her spirit and mental strength, her emotions unstable and unreliable. Sometimes she would feel at peace with the world, with herself, confident that in the end she would adjust and make a good life for herself. Then something would happen, throwing her into spasms of grief, and bitterness would haunt her for days.

Never before had she noticed how many pregnant women walked the earth, even here in a country with a near-zero population growth. They were everywhere—in the bank, the supermarket, McDonalds. And as ubiquitous were the babies, sitting in shopping carts, in strollers, on their mothers' hips. Curly-haired babies and bald-headed ones, thin ones and chubby ones. Babies that looked wide-eyed and serious, or gurgling and smiling, and Faye had never before realised how different they all looked.

Why had she never noticed before? Why had she never noticed before that baby articles were sold almost everywhere she went? Rattles and plastic pants and jars of baby food and disposable diapers caught her eye everywhere she turned.

She told herself she was sick, unbalanced and should do what Doctor Martin had told her to do—see a psychiatrist and learn to deal with reality and get rid of her morbid obsession with pregnancy and babies. After all, motherhood was not the only way to a fulfilling life. Some women might argue that it was no way at all to have a fulfilling life. In this day and age women could make choices, had options. And she was one of the lucky ones with a profession that could offer her a meaningful and interesting career if she played it right.

Oh, yes, she had all the arguments and all the reasons and rationalisations, but her emotional turmoil remained untouched by them. In those moments of grief all she knew was a sense of loss, pain, emptiness.

Ten days after Kai had left Faye had a phone call, a pleasant male voice belonging to a man named Tom Finley. He had just come back from Nicaragua, he told her. He had spoken with Kai, he said.

'You were in Nicaragua? You talked to Kai?'

The man laughed. 'I was and I did. A lot of people are in Nicaragua these days. The revolution took its toll and there's a lot of work to do.'

'Yes, yes, of course.'

'We were staying in the same hotel,' he continued. 'We've known each other for a long time, but hadn't met for quite a while. Anyway, why I'm calling you is this. Kai told me you're looking for a job, and if you're still available I'd like to talk to you about a position we have opening up here.'

Faye was incredulous, but managed to gather her composure and ask some intelligent questions. She knew she sounded businesslike, professional and confident, and she was pleased with herself.

An appointment was made and Faye was instructed to send in a résumé and some samples of her work in

French, English and Spanish, so they could be studied before the interview.

From the few particulars given over the phone, it sounded as if the job was an interesting one, but Faye was too down-to-earth to let excitement carry her too far. Still, the idea that someone was interested in interviewing her was uplifting and for the rest of the day she felt a kind of hope, a glimmer of light.

That night she was jarred out of sleep by yet another phone call. She jumped out of bed and ran down the stairs to the kitchen, getting there just ahead of Chuck, who looked sleepy and befuddled and was muttering incoherently. Why he didn't have an extension upstairs Faye would never understand.

Strange sounds crackled along the wire, echoing. Then a female voice, rattling off the phone number in Spanish and was that correct?

Finally Kai's voice sounded in her ear and Faye's heart lurched in sudden panic.

'Kai! Is something wrong?'

Laughter. 'No. Did I wake the whole house?'

Relief flooded her. 'No, just Chuck. You want to talk to him?'

'Hell, no. Whatever for? I want to talk to you. Tell him to go to bed.'

Faye turned to Chuck. 'Kai says you can go back to bed.'

Chuck made a horrible grimace. 'Thanks a lot!' he said sarcastically. 'If this isn't an emergency, ask him if he's crazy to call at this hour of the night!'

Faye relayed the question and Kai laughed. 'If it makes him feel any better, tell him yes.'

Face expressionless, she turned to Chuck. 'Kai says yes.'

Chuck scowled and walked away, swearing under his breath.

'Why are you calling?' Faye asked, sinking down on

the cold tile floor and resting her back against one of the cupboards. 'Why are you calling at this hour of the night? It's three o'clock!'

'Two,' he said levelly.

Faye smiled. 'Okay, two for you and three for me. Makes no difference. Aren't you in bed?'

'Sure I am.' A slight pause. 'I was dreaming of you,' he said softly. 'I wanted to hear your voice. Now. I couldn't wait.'

Warmth spread through her and she no longer felt the coldness of the floor, no longer was she aware of her surroundings. She hugged her knees and closed her eyes. 'Oh, Kai. . . .' she said huskily. 'I. . . .' her voice trailed away and she swallowed at a constriction in her throat, seeing in her mind his face, his smiling eyes, knowing no words to say. She missed him. She missed him so much.

'Faye? Are you still there?'

She swallowed again. 'Yes.'

He was thousands of miles away in Managua, a city badly damaged by revolution. She remembered seeing pictures of the destruction on TV. Somewhere in a hotel room on the outskirts of town, Kai was dreaming about her. It gave her the most curious sensation.

'Faye, I miss you. I wish you were here with me, in my bed, in my arms.'

'Yes,' she whispered, 'so do I.' The words had come on their own accord. Her heart was thudding and she was aware of what she had said and it didn't matter because it was true. She felt strangely tremulous, as if he were there right in front of her, looking at her, touching her.

'Faye?' His voice was like a velvet touch across the wire. 'Oh, Faye, you're too damn far away!'

She pressed the receiver tightly against her ear, as if it could make him any closer. 'Yes, I know.'

Just hearing his voice was evoking all manner of

emotions in her, a yearning to reach out to him, touch him. She wanted to be close to him, feel his warmth, have his arms around her.

'You're not angry that I woke you up?'

She smiled. 'No, of course not.'

'I'll be home in another week, eight days to be exact. Will you come and pick me up?'

'I'll be there.' It sounded like a confession—*I'll be there because I can't wait to see you again.* She sensed Kai felt the same, for he said no more except a quiet goodnight, his voice a little husky. Faye replaced the receiver, aware of a curious sense of exhilaration. It remained with her until she drifted away in sweet drowsiness followed by quiet sleep.

A few days later she went to New York for the interview and came away with the feeling that she had made a favourable impression on Tom Finley and that there was a real chance she would be offered the job. The company was small, and its business was developing specialised educational material in French, Spanish and English, mostly designed for overseas use. The job was exciting, with potential for advancement and diversification, and ample opportunity to be creative and use her own judgment.

As Faye roamed through Manhattan that afternoon, thinking and considering, she became increasingly enthusiastic. It would be a change. It would be interesting. And working in New York had its appeal, too. Everything seemed so perfect. The office was located only a short distance from Grand Central Station. She could take the train in and walk the rest of the way and not worry about bus and subway schedules, or the expense of daily taxi rides.

She felt good and her step was light as she walked on. New York was exciting. *If* she got the job. . . . Two weeks before she would know. A sense of expectation filled her, an excitement she hadn't felt for a long time. There was something to look forward to, to hope for. For the moment at least it was battling her lethargic mood, the apathy that dominated her outlook on life so much of the time.

Faye caught the four-five train home. She stared out the window, thinking, making plans. *If* she got the job. . . .

She felt better, so much better. And in three days Kai would come home. She looked forward to seeing him again, being with him, listening to his slow easy tone, seeing his laughing blue eyes.

Saturday finally came and Faye zipped down the turnpike in Kai's car. She was early, much too early, and the waiting dragged. She had a cup of coffee and ate a piece of apple pie with phoney whipped cream on top. She wandered around the endless corridors, back and forth, because she couldn't sit still. She counted the flags lining the balcony, and watched the people coming and going.

Intermittently she stared at the arrival schedule, willing it to indicate the arrival of Kai's flight from Miami. It did so, finally, and Faye gave an involuntary sigh, hearing at the same time the announcement over the crackling p.a. system.

The first thing she noticed was his faithful Stetson, way up above the other passengers' heads, and her heart lurched drunkenly. Next she saw his darkly tanned face and the blue, blue eyes, and everything around her faded away into nothingness.

She saw only Kai now—his tall, lean body, his casual, easygoing stride. Jacket slung over his shoulder, he moved forward, looking, searching the crowd.

All she was aware of was him, his face, and the light that sprang up in his eyes as his searching gaze met hers.

CHAPTER FIVE

She was in his arms, wrapped up so tightly against him she could barely breathe. Her face was pressed against his chest and she could hear the strong, solid beating of his heart and smell the warm male scent of his body. After a moment Kai lifted her face and kissed her hard, then put her away from him a little, looking down at her, smiling.

'How have you been?'

'Okay,' she said without enthusiasm.

'Miss me?'

Faye lowered her eyes. 'Yes,' she said a little huskily.

He pulled her close again and kissed her, more gently this time. Then he released her, picked up his jacket that had slid to the ground and slung it back over his shoulder. He looked at her with a deep glitter in his eyes and his hand reached out and touched her mouth.

'This is a public place and I'll behave,' he said softly. 'Let's get out of here.' He picked up his bags and started towards the exit. In the parking lot he fished his keys out of his pocket and opened the trunk of the car.

Faye took out the extra set of keys he had given her and held them out for him to take. 'Here,' she said, 'your keys.'

He glanced at her hand. 'Keep them,' he said, waving his hand in dismissal. He threw his bags in the trunk and slammed it shut.

She slid into the passenger's seat and looked at him

hesitantly. 'I don't know if I want to go around with your car keys in my pocket,' she said uncertainly.

'Why not?' he asked casually. 'You might as well, if you're going to use my car.' He started the engine and drove out the parking lot.

Faye said nothing and stared down on the keys still in her hand. He was right, of course, but still she was not quite comfortable with his offer. Sooner or later she would have to get herself another car, but first she would have to find a job. Her little yellow Fiat had been written off in the accident. When she had come out of the hospital, her father had loaned her his car, since he had a company car for his own use.

The first few weeks she had been scared to drive, afraid at every curve in the road that another maniac would come crashing into her, but fear had faded, if not completely vanished.

She looked at Kai, and his hand reached out to hers, closing her fingers around the keys.

'Put them away,' he said firmly.

Faye dropped them into her bag and smiled. 'Thank you. You're much too nice.' *Too nice for his own good*, Mrs Brown had said.

He grinned. 'Being nice pays off, at least that's my experience.'

'Did it pay off in Nicaragua?'

One eyebrow rose in question. 'How do you mean that?'

Faye shrugged lightly. 'I'd imagine that Nicaragua is full of dark-haired, dark-eyed beauties waiting to fall all over some blue-eyed blond cowboy from America. Didn't you have a good time?'

He gave her a long, hard look. 'No. As a matter of fact I was very bored.'

'*Bored?*' she asked incredulously.

'Exactly. Haven't you any idea how totally uninteresting it is to sit in a hotel for three weeks?'

'Well, maybe if you're in Nowhere, Nebraska, but not when you're in a place like Managua!'

'A hotel is a hotel, even in Managua.' He threw her a quick, ironic look. 'You think travel is stimulating, exciting, exotic, don't you?'

'Of course I do! I was in Mexico last year and I found it *very* stimulating and exciting and exotic!'

He sighed. 'Oh, the enthusiasm of the innocent!'

'Yes,' she said coolly, 'it must be hard to take for someone as old and blasé as you.'

His eyes narrowed, but he didn't reply, and Faye had the gratifying feeling that she had scored a point.

'Wasn't there anything exciting to do in Managua at all?'

'I went to the movies a lot. Does that count?'

Faye smiled. 'No. What else did you do, besides go to the movies?'

'I worked,' he said dryly. 'And that I enjoyed very much. I was out of town most days, talking to the farmers, checking things out.'

'You mean to tell me that you didn't even come across any nice señoritas willing to spend time with you?' she asked.

'Of course I did,' he said levelly. 'But I wasn't interested.'

'Really? Mrs Brown says you're a ladies' man. A playboy.'

'Oh?' He raised his eyebrows, giving no further comment.

'What happened to all those women who are always flocking around you, according to her? I haven't seen a single one since I met you.'

'I thought you weren't terribly concerned,' he said dryly.

'I'm not,' she said with cool hauteur. 'Just curious.'

'I see. Good old feminine curiosity,' he drawled.

'Oh, go chew a rock!' she flung at him, giving an exasperated laugh.

He looked wounded. 'I might break my teeth.'

She smiled her sweetest smile. 'I know.'

Kai sighed heavily. 'What are we fighting about, anyway?'

'About the other women in your life. About your reputation as a ladies' man. Mrs Brown keeps warning me. She keeps dropping hints.'

'Are you worried about it?'

'About what?'

'The other women in my life.'

Faye suppressed a laugh, but only barely. 'No, I'm not terribly concerned.'

He groaned. 'Good. I wouldn't want you to be.'

Faye looked at him. She still had no answer to her original question. And she wanted one, if it took her all night.

'What happened to them, anyway?'

He threw her a blank stare. 'To whom?'

'The other women in your life. The ones that always flock around you—according to Mrs Brown.'

'Oh, them.' He gave her a slow grin, then looked back on the road. A minute passed, then another. Faye waited. Then he looked at her again, smiling, but something had changed in his eyes—subtly, almost imperceptibly.

'I got rid of them,' he said with faint emphasis. 'I had no use for them any more.' His hand touched hers briefly. 'I found you,' he added on a low note.

For a moment Faye didn't know what to say, or how to interpret the meaning of his words. Somewhere deep inside her they had touched off a spark of sudden fear, a faint trepidation.

'That's a nice compliment,' she said at last, trying to sound casual..

'It's meant to be.'

'Thank you.'

Faye wondered what he was thinking, but couldn't even guess. She moved her eyes away from his face and stared outside, watching the cars going past. Lots of complaints about the rising price of gasoline, but few people were actually slowing down to conserve fuel. She strained to read a sticker on the rear bumper of a car. *Insanity is hereditary. You get it from your kids.*

Well, Faye thought wryly, one more thing I don't have to worry about. She closed her eyes, briefly, then straightened in her seat.

'Tom Finley called me,' she said after a pause.

Kai gave her a quick, sideways glance. 'I hope you don't mind I told him about you, but it seemed too good an opportunity to miss.'

Faye laughed. 'I'm not proud. Besides, I'm hardly getting the job thrown at me. I'm going through the system like all the other applicants, and they do have others on their list of prospects.'

'But you'll be right there on the top, is my guess. With your knowledge of two languages and your experience and . . . er . . . my most enthusiastic recommendation. . . .'

Faye gave him a level look, noticed the laughter in his eyes. 'Do you know him that well?'

'Well enough that it makes a difference. We did some work together several years ago.'

'So . . .' she said slowly, 'if I get the job, I'll have to give you some credit and I'll be in your debt.'

He smiled blissfully. 'Correct.'

'And you're going to demand a pay-off?'

'Right again.'

Faye sighed dramatically. 'You're horrible. You take advantage of me,' she complained.

'And you love every minute of it.'

The toll booths saved her from a reply, and the subject was changed.

'The children invited you for Sunday dinner,' she told him, 'but I warn you, I'm cooking.'

'What's wrong with your cooking?'

'I cheat.'

'You're calling out for a pizza,' he stated, looking resigned.

'I'm just a little more subtle than that,' she said, laughing. 'Let's just say I raided the frozen food section at the Grand Union yesterday. But I'll put all of it in our own pots and pans, so nobody will know.'

'Except me.'

'It'll be our secret,' she said gravely.

He sighed heavily. 'Of all the secrets I'd like to have with you, this isn't one of them.'

Which didn't surprise her in the least. Neither did it surprise her when he drove straight to his house without taking her home first. She wanted to be with him and she wasn't going to think beyond that.

Kai showered and changed while Faye put on some music and busied herself in the kitchen making an omelette for both of them. Someone had stocked the refrigerator with fresh foods, presumably the lady who came in to do the housework once a week.

She heard him enter the kitchen and turned around to face him. Wearing jeans and a fitted Western sports shirt, he leaned against the door post with nonchalant grace, thumbs hooked behind his belt. The blue eyes regarded her intensely, as if he was taking in every detail of her appearance—her face, her body, everything.

'Come here, Faye,' he said, and there was a huskiness in his voice that flooded her with a peculiar sensation and slowly she took a step towards him, her heart suddenly thumping wildly.

She didn't understand what it was about him that made her act so strangely, as if she had no control at all over her own reactions, as if she were merely a puppet on a string and all he had to do was pull the string and make her do whatever he wanted.

He straightened away from the door, took her in his arms and began to kiss her, fiercely, and without any restraint. She answered him with a yearning that sprang up from unknown depths and it was wonderful and intoxicating for a few precious moments, then it faded away and she was filled with a nameless fear. Something was happening and she didn't understand it. Strength drained from her body and the weakness of tears invaded her. Her legs began to tremble and she was afraid, so afraid she wanted to run, but all she could do was cling to him, hold him.

'Faye,' he whispered against her lips, 'Faye, I missed you. I was thinking about you, dreaming about you all the time.'

She didn't answer, couldn't speak. He lifted her face, but she closed her eyes, afraid to look at him.

'Look at me, Faye.'

She shook her head, lowering it.

'What's wrong?' he asked softly, his hand stroking her hair.

'I don't know,' she whispered, the words almost sticking in her throat, and she felt strange and terrible and she wanted to weep.

'Are you afraid of me?'

Again she shook her head, wordlessly, not trusting her voice. She wasn't afraid of him, but of something else, something ominous and threatening. Something undefinable and elusive.

'I would never hurt you, Faye. Please trust me.'

She nodded silently.

Kai lifted her chin and kissed her closed eyes—gently, so gently, she could barely feel his touch, only

the warmth of his lips. Then his arm went around her
shoulder and he led her to a chair at the kitchen table.

'Let's eat.'

The odd, fearful feeling faded as they ate, and small
talk took over with the familiar banter going back and
forth between them. They took their coffee to the
living room. Kai built a fire and they sat on the floor
in front of it, watching the flames in silence.

After a while he put his cup down and took her
hand.

'It isn't working very well, is it?' he asked quietly,
still looking into the fire.

'What isn't?'

He looked at her then and there was no laughter in
his eyes. 'That little game of pretence we've been playing for the last few weeks—the playboy and the play-
girl act. Fun and games and everything light and
superficial.'

'I didn't know we were pretending,' said Faye,
trying to sound casual, but inside her apprehension
stirred.

He gave her a searching look. 'You've been playing
the role of a lighthearted seductive little flirt, and
you're not, Faye. I know you're not.'

She smiled innocently. 'I'm not?' she asked, refusing to match his serious tone.

'Stop pretending,' he said, looking straight at her.

She was silent. Averting her eyes, she looked down
on her hands clasped together in her lap.

'You're not the kind of girl a man has an affair with,
Faye. You're the kind of girl a man falls in love with.'

Fear suddenly overwhelmed her—a fear so strange
and incomprehensible, she was helpless to fight it. She
swallowed painfully, not looking at him.

'Don't,' she said tonelessly.

'Don't what?'

'Fall in love with me.'

There was a heavy silence, and after a few interminable moments Faye glanced up at him uneasily. He was studying her, a curious expression in his blue eyes. Then he shook his head.

'That's the strangest request I've ever had in my life. What would be so bad about me falling in love with you?'

The atmosphere in the room was much too serious for comfort. She didn't like this conversation, and she tried to smile, tried to inject it with a little frivolity.

'It would be disastrous,' she said airily, hoping desperately he would leave the conversation at that, accept it in the way she was presenting it.

There was a significant pause, but she kept smiling at him, willing him to smile back at her. He did, finally, a ghost of a smile touching his lips.

'Of course,' he said, his light tone matching hers. 'You're a dangerous woman. You'd break my heart.'

She felt almost faint with relief.

'You're right,' she said. 'I just wanted to warn you.'

His mouth was smiling back at her, but in his eyes she found no sparkle and no laughter.

The evening was spoiled. A strangeness had invaded the atmosphere, intangible, and Faye felt ill at ease. On the surface nothing had changed, but underneath, a restraint and a guardedness stifled their words and actions.

It was still early when she asked him to take her home and he did so without a word of protest. He kissed her goodnight at the door, a friendly, undemanding kiss, and left her without coming in. In the hall she took off her jacket, feeling miserable with regret—regret for something she didn't even understand. She had wanted to apologise to Kai, but she wasn't sure for what, and so she had said nothing.

Chuck was in the living room, watching television, and after a word of greeting Faye sat down and fixed her eyes on the set. There was no way in the world she would be able to sleep, so she might as well stay up for a while.

Chuck glanced at her. 'Where's Kai? He did make it back today, didn't he?'

Faye nodded. 'I picked him up. He didn't come in because he's tired.' The lie rolled out with surprising ease.

Chuck searched her face. 'What's wrong? You look as if you've gambled away your last cent.'

She forced a smile. 'Nothing is wrong. You worry too much about me.'

Chuck's dark eyes didn't leave her face. 'Do I?' he asked quietly. 'Sometimes I wonder if I worry enough. I know my little sister, and I can tell when she's hurting.'

There was a lump in her throat, and she lowered her eyes and looked at the clenched hands in her lap. After a moment's silence she took a deep breath and met his gaze.

'Chuck . . . I . . . I'm trying to work out something by myself, but I can't talk about it.' She swallowed, not looking away. 'I'll have to do this myself, but I'll be all right. Really I will.' There was a conviction in her voice she didn't feel, and from the look on Chuck's face she knew that he wasn't so sure, either.

'Faye, it helps just talking about a problem. It can't be good to lock it all up inside you and let it ferment there. It only makes things worse.' There was a persuasive quality to his voice. He was worried about her and he wanted her to talk about it, she knew, but she couldn't. Not now, not yet. Again her hands clenched together, helplessly, and she stared down on them miserably.

'I'm not ready to talk about it yet,' she said tonelessly. 'I just wish that you wouldn't worry about me.' She didn't want him to worry because it made her feel guilty. She didn't want him to think she didn't trust him. He was her brother and she loved him and she didn't want to cause him any distress.

Silence followed her words and Faye could feel his speculative regard, his silent deliberation. After a moment he let out a sigh of resignation. 'Okay, we'll leave it for the time being. Would you like a drink?'

'Yes, please,' she said, smiling at him with relief. 'I'd like some apricot brandy.'

Chuck grimaced. 'You and my mother-in-law!'

Faye laughed. 'That's the first negative comment I've heard about your mother-in-law. Does she drink it too?'

'That's why I have it. And that's her only flaw as far as I'm concerned.'

'And you cater to it.'

'You'd better believe it!' He grinned. 'I know a good thing when I see it. And Elizabeth is as good as they come. I have to keep her on my side.'

He had been lucky, Faye knew. Despite their own grief at the loss of their daughter, Chuck's in-laws had supported and helped him without taking over and running his life for him. Living in the same town, being so close at hand had been a blessing, and still was. Faye had got to know them well now that she lived with Chuck and the children, and she could do nothing but like them.

'I want to ask you a favour,' said Chuck as he handed her her drink and sat down. 'Do you have any special plans for next weekend?'

Faye shook her head. 'No.'

He swirled his drink about in his glass and looked at her. 'I'd like to go away for the weekend. Without the children.'

'I'll stay home with them.'

'Are you sure you can manage them all by yourself?'

Faye grinned. 'You make it sound as if it's a monumental task!'

'They'll try and take advantage of your soft heart,' he said soberly.

'Don't worry, I'll manage.' She took a sip from her drink. 'Where are you going? Or shouldn't I ask?'

He gave her a lopsided grin. 'I don't know where I'm going and I don't particularly care.'

Faye looked at him thoughtfully. 'Are you going to tell me about it or do I have to drag it out of you?'

'Try dragging,' he said, laughing.

'You're going away with a woman, I can guess that much. Only why haven't I met her? I've been here for weeks.'

'She wasn't here. She just came back from Europe.'

'Do the children know her?'

'They met her once.'

'No overkill on that score,' she said dryly.

'I don't like them to get any ideas before I do.' He grimaced. 'Any female that comes into this house more than once is invited by Darci to stay on for the rest of her life.'

'She wants a mother,' Faye stated quietly.

Chuck nodded. 'I have to be careful.'

Faye took another sip of her apricot brandy and studied Chuck's face. Since Anne's death he had aged considerably. Now there was a touch of grey in his dark hair, but it seemed to enhance his good looks. He and Anne had been very happy together and Faye would like to see him happy again. He was a fine man and a good father, but finding a loving wife was no easy task, and putting pressure on him was the wrong thing to do, so she made no further comment.

The next morning she woke up feeling exhausted. She was aware of a feeling of painful regret when she thought of the previous night. Something had happened to spoil the evening. She had looked forward to it for a long time and somehow it had all gone wrong. She remembered Kai's phone call from Nicaragua—the longing in his voice, the tenderness as he had spoken her name. She remembered, too, her own emotions at that time and a faint, panicky feeling stirred. Something unexpected was happening, something she had no control over.

For a few moments she lay in bed, not able to move. Don't let it be true, she thought. Please don't let it be true.

The morning was a blur. In the afternoon she fixed dinner and put it in the oven. She was washing tomatoes under the tap when she saw Kai striding along the flagstone path through the yard. The first thing she noticed was the brilliant splash of colour on his chest—the tie, Darci's tie. Faye groaned inwardly. He was wearing it; he was really wearing it. Except for the tie he looked immaculate in his tailored pants and jacket. He carried a bunch of flowers wrapped in green tissue paper and suddenly her heart was in her throat. Please, she thought, please don't let him give me roses.

Suddenly from nowhere the children came racing toward him across the lawn. Kai bent down on his haunches and talked to them. She heard them laugh, then he fished something out of his pocket and gave it to them—a toy, it seemed. Something with a small ball on a string, very brightly coloured. Darci kissed him soundly on the cheeks in thanks and for a while he helped them with the toy, demonstrating how to use it.

Looking through the window, Faye watched them, suddenly seeing everything through a wet mist. The water was running uselessly over her fingers as she stared outside. Blooming azaleas, blue sky, green grass—brilliant colours of a happy spring day. And Kai was part of it with his pink and purple tie he wore to please little Darci. He loved those two, she knew. He wanted some of his own, he'd said. He was going back to Texas one day and raise kids and crops. Faye could see it in her mind's eye. Dusty, barren desert land he would turn into fertile soil producing food crops. A low white ranch house. Children. A couple of dogs. Horses. A woman.

In the imaginary picture she couldn't visualise the woman. She was merely a shape, a silhouette without distinguishing colours or features. But the children she could see very clearly. They looked like him, blue-eyed and blond, tall with slender limbs, wearing boots and jeans and wide-brimmed hats. She had had visions like this before, but never quite so clearly. She blinked her eyes dry, furiously, saw Kai coming towards the back door leading into the kitchen. She turned off the water and dried the tomatoes on a paper towel. The door opened.

'Howdy, ma'am!'

She turned and smiled. 'Hi.'

With a theatrical gesture and a little bow he handed her the flowers. 'Flowers for the cook,' he drawled.

Daisies, white with gold centres. Simple, straight-forward, unpretentious daisies. They were lovely and she smiled at him, pleased.

'Thank you!'

He came a little closer, put his hands on her shoulders and looked into her eyes. '*Thank you* is not enough,' he said, his voice low and provoking. Faye noticed the laughter in his eyes and suddenly she felt happy again, relieved somehow that he wasn't angry with her, or disappointed, although she couldn't put into words why he should be. Last night . . . she didn't want to think about last night. It was forgotten now and she wanted to go on the way it had been.

Standing on her toes, she kissed him on the cheek. Immediately his arms went around her, gathering her close to him. 'You didn't think you could get away with just that, did you?' he whispered close to her ear.

She shook her head, her face moving against his tie. No, she knew what was coming. She wanted him close to her, she always wanted that, to hear his heart beat, feel the warmth of him, smell the clean smell of his skin. His mouth searched for hers and found it, and a lightheadedness invaded her at the feel of the warm firmness of his lips on hers.

'Faye,' he whispered, 'don't tease me, for God's sake! We're in the kitchen!'

She stood very still, feeling and hearing her heart beating wildly. She looked up and met his eyes. He was smiling, but there was a puzzled expression on his face.

'I don't know what the hell to make of you, Faye,' he said, shaking his head.

A sound made them look away, and Faye noticed Darci standing in the doorway studying them with interest.

'Hello Darci,' Kai said calmly. He didn't move away from Faye, but held his arm firmly around her.

'I'm hungry,' Darci complained, still looking from Faye to Kai and back.

'We'll be eating soon,' Faye answered.

Darci's eyes, dark and solemn, looked at Kai. 'Is Auntie Faye your girl-friend now?'

Kai looked back, equally solemn. 'Yes, she is.'

Faye grew warm. It was absolutely ridiculous to feel this way, but the tone of his voice was grave and serious as if he were making a promise or a pledge.

'I'm never going to be anybody's girl-friend,' Darci vowed.

'Why not?' Kai looked at Darci with amusement and Faye laughed.

Darci wrinkled her nose. 'I don't like all that mushy mushy stuff. Kissing on the lips, yuk!' She turned and dashed out the door, and Kai roared with laughter.

'Where does she get ideas like that?'

Faye shrugged lightly and smiled. 'They come naturally when you're six.' Every time Darci saw people kissing on TV she made faces as if it was the most revolting thing in the world, and Faye's explanations had done nothing to soften her response.

'I'm glad you're not six,' Kai stated, and kissed her, very firmly, on the lips. 'Now, what can I do to help with dinner?'

'Nothing. It's in the oven and will be ready in fifteen minutes. All I have to do is cut the tomatoes for the salad.'

The food was good and everyone ate with appetite. But the children were restless and after they had finished Chuck suggested a hike through the Nature Centre.

'Let's all go,' Joey decided, but Kai shook his head. 'I'll help Auntie Faye clear up the dishes.'

'And I'll get your dessert ready,' said Faye.

The children raced out the door and Chuck followed them. 'We won't be more than an hour or so,' he said as he closed the door.

It didn't take long to clear away the dishes and stack them in the dishwasher. They worked quickly and efficiently together and when it was done Faye filled the coffee-maker and Kai found mugs, sugar and milk.

'Do you play backgammon?' he asked, and the question surprised her. She hadn't expected him to like to play games. Well, she thought wryly, at least not that kind of game.

After a slight hesitation, she shook her head. 'No.' It wasn't exactly the truth. She knew how to play, but it had been more than a year since she'd last looked at a backgammon board. She hadn't been a good player, hadn't played often enough to give her enough experience. A refresher course by Kai certainly would do no harm.

'I'll teach you,' he said. 'It's easy to learn, the rules

are simple.' He poured the coffee and took the cups to the living room. From a shelf in the bookcase he took a backgammon set and put it on the table. He arranged the pieces on the board and proceeded to explain the game.

Slowly Faye moved through the first game, carefully making moves, embarrassed now by her pretended ignorance. She lost, but only barely.

Kai said nothing, concentrated on the game, but when it was all over, he directed his gaze to her face and studied her with narrowed eyes.

'Very good,' he drawled.

She smiled up at him innocently. 'I'm a fast learner.'

His blue eyes glinted ominously. 'The hell you are,' he said on a low note.

'What's the matter?' she asked lightly. 'Are you a sore loser?'

'No, *you're* a bad liar.'

She assumed an air of shocked indignation, knowing full well she couldn't fool him. It was a game, a silly little game of pretence, but she enjoyed it.

'You may not be an experienced player,' he said slowly, 'but this certainly wasn't the first time you ever played backgammon.' There was a menacing look in his eyes and she watched him as he slowly got up from his chair, his eyes holding hers. 'You're going to have to pay for that,' he said softly.

He came towards her and Faye jumped to her feet and ran. He was too fast for her and she didn't even make it out of the room. His arm shot out and pulled her to him and Faye couldn't contain her laughter any longer. She tried to struggle loose, but did so more for effect than with any hope of succeeding. Kai's arms tightened around her with unrelenting strength.

'You can't escape me,' he said softly, very softly, 'so don't try.'

There was a strange silence and the laughter inside her died. There was something in the tone of his voice and something in the way he looked at her that made the fear surface in her again. *You can't escape me.* He wasn't talking about just now, he was talking about something deeper, something unspoken, but very real.

She stood in his arms, motionless, not knowing what to say. His hands reached up to touch her cheeks and then her hair, tipping her head back. 'Don't look at me like that,' he said in an odd, controlled voice. And then he kissed her, not gently, but with a fierce possessiveness that made her senses reel. There was a hunger in his touch that stirred up in her a deep primitive yearning.

When finally he pulled back, Faye was breathless and trembling on her legs, her heart pounding. She looked at Kai and saw unexpected laughter in the clear blue of his eyes, and he smiled at her—a complacent little smile.

'You never fight me,' he said, a touch of humour in his voice.

Her cheeks grew warm, but she didn't avert her eyes. 'I can't help myself,' she said, resignation in her voice. 'You're irresistible and I'm putty in your hands.'

He laughed softly. 'Aren't I lucky?'

'Mmmm . . . very. I'm not usually so . . . er . . . accommodating, so easily charmed.'

'Swept off your feet, bowled over.'

'That too.' She smiled sweetly. 'And you're unbearably arrogant and presumptuous and. . . .'

He silenced her with a kiss. 'I don't want to hear your insults,' he murmured against her lips. 'It makes me want to do terrible things to you to punish you.'

'Like what?'

'Like kidnap you and hold you hostage in a deserted mountain cabin for an entire week.'

Laughter bubbled up inside her again. 'As long as you didn't forget the candles and the wine and the music I wouldn't mind.'

His eyes narrowed as he studied her face. 'Don't tempt me.'

'You just happen to know a deserted mountain cabin, right?'

'No, but believe me, I'd have no trouble finding one.'

'Well, I couldn't let you do that. As a consultant your time is too valuable, I know that.'

'There are more important things in life than work and making money.'

'Such as?'

'Taking kids to Disney World. Going camping in the woods and listening to the birds. Spending a week in a deserted mountain cabin with a girl with freckles.'

'You have to be able to afford all that.'

'I'm lucky, I can. Also it depends on what priorities you have in life.'

'And whether you marry a woman who demands furs and jewels and fancy world cruises.'

Kai grimaced. 'Not my type.'

'What's your type?' She couldn't resist asking.

'Mmm, let me think.' His eyes were full of laughing lights, like tiny blue candles. 'I like the soft and sweet and funny type.' He was still standing very close to her, his arms around her, and he moved them up, curling his fingers through her hair. His mouth touched her cheek, caressingly, moved to her ear. 'Someone like you,' he whispered. 'And I'd keep her in the kitchen, barefoot and pregnant.'

Faye's heart made a sickening lurch and for a terrifying moment it seemed as if she couldn't breathe, as if she were suffocating in his arms. She stood very still, her mind in panic, looking for something to say.

'You don't find women like that any more. They

belong in the last century,' she said as casually as she could. She moved out of his arms, smiled bravely, shaking her head. 'Kai Ellington, you shock me! You sound like a male chauvinist of the worst kind. I'm going to pour myself another cup of coffee. Would you like one?'

She picked up the coffee cups and walked into the kitchen, not waiting for a reply. She leaned against the counter, staring at the coffee pot. She was trembling so badly she didn't dare pick it up. Oh, God, she thought, don't let it be true. Don't let him be serious about all this. I didn't want this, I can't handle it! A man like him. . . . Fragments of conversations came back to her—memories of the things he had told her about his plans for the future. Visions whirled through her mind—a low ranch house under the hot Texas sun, blond, blue-eyed children riding horses, fields of growing wheat. . . .

She heard him enter the kitchen and fear engulfed her, making her legs almost buckle beneath her. She grasped the edge of the counter and closed her eyes, willing herself to calm down, to relax her taut nerves. And then Kai was behind her, drawing her against him, his arms around her waist, his face in her hair.

'Faye,' he said quietly, 'I love you.'

CHAPTER SIX

FAYE'S throat was locked and she couldn't utter a sound. There was a deep, bitter pain inside her. *No!* she cried inwardly, don't say it! Please don't say it!

But Kai had said it and now it was too late. Too late to pull back and run, too late to cover up. It was out in the open, and the word was love.

She hadn't meant it to happen. A man like Kai was not for her—not for ever, not for keeps. All she wanted was an innocent lighthearted romance, no strings attached. On the surface that was exactly what it was, what it seemed to be. But underneath all the games and jokes and banter another truth had been hiding, and now it was surfacing. The game of pretence was over.

She stood in his arms, very still, silent, not speaking. His lips caressed her cheek. 'Faye,' he said softly, 'I mean that.'

'I know.' Her voice was barely a whisper and nothing more would come. He turned her around to face him and she met his gaze with numb despair. More than anything else she wanted to put her head on his shoulder and say, 'I love you too,' but there was no way she could utter those words, no way in the world she could be serious about a man like Kai. He was a man with dreams she could never be part of, hopes and expectations she could never fulfil.

For a long moment he studied her face, his eyes serious, wondering.

'You look as if I'd given you the death sentence,' he said at last. 'Don't you have anything to say?'

Her eyes filled with tears. 'I'm sorry,' she said, and her voice shook. She didn't want to cry now, give herself away in a moment of weakness. 'I'm sorry ... I hadn't expected this to happen. I can't ... I don't. ...' Helplessly she clenched her hands into fists. 'I can't handle it right now. I ... I don't want to get into something I. ...'

'... can't get out of?' Kai gave a faint little smile that held no amusement.

'Yes.'

'You thought we were having a little romantic fling, nothing serious.' His voice was flat.

'Yes,' she whispered miserably.

'That's why you didn't want to hear what I had to say last night. It scared you.'

Faye nodded, looking away. The words he had said were crystal clear in her mind. '*You're not the kind of girl a man has an affair with, Faye. You're the kind of girl a man falls in love with.*'

And he had. She had felt it coming and ignored the signs. Kai was a charmer, a ladies' man, a love 'em and leave 'em type, and she had clung to that image in spite of the evidence that this time for him it was different.

His face came closer and he kissed her gently, very gently as if to assure her of her safety. His lips were warm and firm, lightly touching hers, then moving to her cheeks, her closed eyes. A small shiver ran along her back and involuntarily her hands rested on his back. He pressed her close against him.

'I love you,' he whispered against her cheek, 'and I'm saying that for no other reason than that it's the truth. Do you think I'm leading you on?'

Faye shook her head. 'No.' Instinctively she knew he wasn't playing games. She believed in his sincerity, blindly. His body felt warm and strong against her, all of him touching her, but somehow she found no comfort in it. She felt tense, her nerves taut, her stomach tight.

'What makes you so afraid, Faye?'

'I'm not . . . I'm not afraid.'

He moved her away from him a little. 'No? Then what is it?'

When she didn't answer he lifted her chin and looked at her with so much love and tenderness that tears welled up in her eyes.

'What's wrong, Faye? Please tell me.'

Oh, God, she prayed, don't let me go to pieces. She took a deep shuddering breath and blinked away her tears.

'Nothing's wrong,' she said tonelessly. 'Only . . . only I wish this . . . this hadn't happened. I wasn't expecting you to fall in love with me.'

'No?' His tone was dry. 'But it has happened, Faye,' he continued on a softer note. 'What was it that you were expecting? What were you expecting of me? Of this relationship?'

She swallowed, didn't look at him. 'Everything. Except . . . except this.'

'Love?'

She nodded wordlessly.

'And now?'

'I don't know.' She didn't know what now, what to do, what to expect.

There was a slight pause. 'Do you want me to leave you alone?'

Her eyes flew to his face. 'No!'

He gave a short mirthless laugh, and his hands dropped away from her shoulders. 'What exactly is it that you want?'

She struggled briefly. She had come this far, now she had to go on. 'I want it to be the way it was before.'

'Good God,' he brought out in a strangled voice, 'I don't believe I'm hearing this!' He turned away from her, staring up at the ceiling, hands jammed into his pockets. 'It won't work. It's ridiculous and you know it.'

Faye said nothing and the silence hung between them like a thick wet mist, cold, impenetrable. Suddenly he swung around and came back to her in two giant strides. His hands came down on her shoulders and he looked into her eyes with a strange, indecipherable emotion.

'Faye, I can't believe we're having this conversation,' he said, his voice very tight, very controlled. 'Were you listening to me? Did you hear what I said? I *love* you, Faye. I've never said that to another woman. What the hell is wrong with that?'

Her heart was pounding and there was a lump in her throat, an ache inside her. 'Nothing. Only . . . only I don't want to get in over my head and . . . and drown.'

'What makes you think you'll drown?'

Her body went rigid, her nerves taut. *Because I can't swim*, she answered silently. And the words were screaming inside her. *I can't swim! I can't swim!*

'What makes you think you'll drown?' he repeated, studying her with narrowed eyes.

She turned away from him. 'I know I would,' she said flatly. 'I just know I would.' She walked out of the kitchen. If ever she should give in, if ever she should admit she loved him, to herself, or to him, only heartbreak would come of it. She could never be the kind of wife he wanted. She could never deprive him of having children of his own. She could never marry him.

In the living room she stared at the fireplace, dark and cold and empty. She hugged herself, shivering. She felt cold, so cold. She heard Kai come into the room and sensed him behind her, and then his arms came around her and he held her tightly, very tightly, until the warmth of his body flowed over into hers and she stopped shivering. Then, gently, he released her.

'I'll get the coffee,' he said.

Chuck and the children came home a while later and Faye made a fresh pot of coffee and cut the strawberry shortcake she had made for dessert. Kai listened to the children, saying little, and she knew that he, too, was preoccupied with other thoughts. He left soon after the cake was eaten and Faye struggled miserably through the rest of the day. She gave the children their baths, watched TV, read a book. At times she was aware of Chuck's searching look, but he said nothing, much to her relief.

She barely slept, dozing at times, haunted by Kai's face, his eyes, the things he had said. In the morning she dragged herself out of bed, but didn't bother to get dressed. She got the children ready for school and helped Chuck cook breakfast. After they'd all left she went back to her room and sat down on the bed. Should she try to sleep some more, or take a shower and get dressed? She felt like a zombie, numb, lifeless.

She took a long, hot shower, but it didn't make her feel any better. Back in her room she took off her robe and looked at herself in the long mirror, like she had done so many times before. And like so many times before the same thoughts came to her mind—a routine, a ritual to purge herself from sorrow and self-pity.

She was alive. She could walk. She could hear and see and eat normally. The scars on her stomach would always be there, but they were fading. She would never have to worry about morning sickness, stretch-marks, C-sections. She'd never have to wash diapers, get out of bed to give a two o'clock feed, or worry about teething or measles or braces or the suitability of babysitters. She'd never need to nurse a guilt complex about her worth as a mother. She could sleep in on weekends. She would be free and live as she wanted, pursue a career, go as she pleased, travel.

Faye stared at herself, hard.

She could never marry a man like Kai.

It was a thought worse than all the others, a pain too great even for tears. She closed the robe and hugged herself, staring at her reflection with unseeing eyes. I'm no good, she thought. I'm no good for a man like Kai. She went over to the bed and lay down. Rolled up into a ball, her knees to her chin, she lay there in numb misery, not moving, not crying.

Sounds somewhere in the silent house dragged her back to consciousness. A door opening, footsteps in the living room. Kai.

'Faye? Faye, where are you?'

She lay motionless, not answering his call. He was knocking on her door now, calling again, and when she didn't answer he pushed open the door and came in.

'Faye!' In two steps he was next to her bed. 'Are you all right? Are you sick?'

She kept her eyes closed. 'I'm fine.'

'Why aren't you dressed? Why are you in bed?'

'I'm tired. I didn't sleep last night.'

A brief silence. 'Well, that makes two of us.' His voice was dry.

Faye said nothing, just lay there, not stirring.

'For God's sake, look at me! Sit up!' He reached for her but she shrank away from him.

'Please leave me alone. I want to sleep.'

'No.' He pulled her up. 'We're going to have a talk, you and I.'

'No! I don't want to talk!' Some of her inertia seemed to leave her. She slid off the bed and walked over to the window, her back turned. 'I told you yesterday I don't want. . . .'

'I *know* what you told me and I've been lying awake

all the damn night thinking about it and I don't buy it! I don't believe that's what you want!

'It can't be any other way.' Her voice shook.

'Explain that to me.'

'No! You'll just have to take my word for it.'

She sensed his frustration, felt the vibrations clear across the room.

'Dammit, Faye! I *love* you! I want to *marry* you!'

'Stop saying that!' She swung around, tears filling her eyes. He was nothing but a blur, still standing near the bed. She was filled with a bitter, helpless anguish and she wanted to scream out in impotent rage. Something inside her snapped and she took a deep, shuddering breath. 'You don't have to say that!' she cried. 'You can have me, don't you know that? You can have me and you don't have to say that you love me, or marry me, or make any kind of promises!' She was near hysteria, convulsive tremors shaking her body. All reason had left her and she couldn't stop herself. 'Here!' She threw off her robe and it slid to the floor, leaving her standing there in front of him, naked. 'Here! You can have me, I'm all yours! Just don't . . . don't. . . .' Her voice broke and sobs racked her body. Through a haze of tears she saw Kai coming towards her. Without a word he picked up the robe and put it around her shoulders and took her in his arms. She began to struggle, wildly, but he held her so tightly that she had to stop. She leaned against him, trembling uncontrollably, tears streaming down her face.

He began to stroke her hair, softly, soothingly, and for a long time he didn't speak, just held her close. Then he kissed her, just a soft brush of his lips. 'Faye, I don't want a give-away. Don't you understand?' His voice seemed to come from far away, barely penetrating layers of bitterness and misery. 'I want you,

Faye—all of you. Your heart and mind and soul, not just your body. I want your love. I want all of you.'

She heard the words, but her mind refused to deal with them, and she couldn't think, couldn't speak. She was tired, so tired. She leaned against him with her eyes closed and it seemed as if all feeling ebbed away, leaving her empty, blank.

He lifted her face to his with both hands and his mouth found hers and he kissed her with an over-powering possessiveness. She had no strength to resist, no strength to respond.

'I want you, Faye.' His voice was very calm, very steady. 'I don't understand what's wrong, but I'm not going to give up, you hear?'

He wanted an answer, but she was incapable of speech. She felt like a limp rag doll, until he took her by the shoulders and gently shook her.

'Did you hear me, Faye?'

She nodded. 'Yes,' she murmured huskily.

'Now, put that damned robe on right.' It was sliding off her shoulders and he helped her put her arms through the sleeves, then swung her up in his arms and carried her to the bed as if she were a small, sick child. He put her down, gently, and covered her with the blankets.

'Now, go to sleep. When Mrs Brown comes in I'll tell her to be quiet.' He left her without waiting for an answer and Faye, miraculously, fell asleep.

It was almost eleven when Faye woke up. She hurried into a pair of slacks and a shirt and quickly pulled a brush through her hair. Why am I hurrying? she wondered suddenly. I don't have to catch a train. She finished on a slower note, putting on make-up and searching for her shoes under the bed. Coffee. She needed coffee.

Mrs Brown was in the kitchen, assembling a big pot of stew—meat, carrots, onions, celery.

'Are you all right?' she asked, looking worried. 'Kai said to let you sleep. You're not coming down with 'flu, are you?'

'No.' Faye forced a wan smile. 'I was just tired. I had a bad night.' She found a mug and poured herself some coffee. 'Anything I can help you with?'

'Not right now, thank you, honey.' Mrs Brown added cut-up carrots to the stew. 'You're such a help all the time, it makes me feel guilty.'

Faye laughed. 'Whatever for?'

Mrs Brown shrugged. 'I'm getting paid to do this work, and you're doing half of it for me.'

'I want to. I can't sit around idly watching you run around and doing it all alone.' She took a knife and cut a big slice of the chocolate cake that was sitting on the counter. She put it on a plate and sat down at the kitchen table to eat it. Mrs Brown gave her a quick look.

'Did you have breakfast?'

Faye nodded and swallowed a bit of cake. It tasted as if it had a million calories. 'Yes, I did.' She laughed. 'I told you, I'm trying to get fat. I have to eat often.' She took another bite and chewed it with relish. 'This is really good. Maybe I'll have another piece.'

Mrs Brown shook her head reprovingly. 'Fat! You don't know what you're talking about.'

'I'm only joking. Just a few more pounds and I'll be happy.' Faye got up and cut another piece of cake. For some crazy, unfathomable reason she was hungry.

'Would you mind checking if Kai wants another cup of coffee?' Mrs Brown asked. 'He's only had one.'

Faye pushed back her chair. 'Okay, I'll get his cup.'

She'd have to face him again sooner or later, and now was as good a time as any. She wanted to apologise, somehow, for her behaviour earlier in the morning. It was incredible that she could have done such a thing—offering herself to him so shamelessly. Oh, God, she thought miserably, I don't know what to say. She stood in front of his door, ready to knock, and the phone rang. She hesitated. Maybe she should wait. Then, before she could move away, she heard Kai's voice exploding in the silent office.

'If that troop of baboons can't get their act together, they can forget it!' He was shouting so loud Faye was sure it could be heard in New York. 'I'm not going anywhere without a signed contract in my pocket! And if I don't have it by Thursday I'm not leaving!'

Silence. He was pacing the floor, she could hear.

'No!' The word shot out like a bullet. 'That whole damned outfit is nothing but a bunch of overrated clerks and incompetent amateurs! And Arnolds is a bastard in the first grade and he can go stew in hell!'

Faye slipped away from the door. No way she was going in there now. Her heart was racing, as if somehow she felt that the tirade was directed against herself. She had hardly recognised his voice. There'd been nothing left of his slow and easy way of talking. His usual Southern drawl had vanished as he had uttered the hard-bitten insults. It was hard to believe that it really had been Kai talking. Kai who was calm, quiet, even-tempered, with the laughing lights in his eyes.

Faye went back to the kitchen. 'I can't disturb him right now,' she said to Mrs Brown. 'He's on the phone.'

She could still hear him, all the way here in the kitchen. Only now she couldn't make out what he said, which was just as well.

Mrs Brown let out a sigh and looked at Faye with relief. 'Oh, my, I thought he was shouting at you.'

Faye laughed. 'At me? No.' She had not been the unlucky recipient of his outburst, but she had the uncomfortable suspicion that she had been the reason for it.

A few moments later Kai strolled lazily into the kitchen, his coffee cup in his hand, and Faye's heart leaped. He looked perfectly calm and composed, relaxed even, and he gave the two of them a perfectly normal smile.

'Howdy,' he drawled. He looked at Faye. 'Did you get some sleep?'

'Yes, I did. I feel much better now, except for my ears.'

Mrs Brown chuckled and Kai frowned. 'Your ears?'

She looked at him serenely. 'They're ringing. I often get that from loud noises.' Again Mrs Brown chuckled.

Kai's eyes narrowed and he gave her a long look. 'You heard me on the phone, I gather.'

'So did the rest of Connecticut. Only I happened to stand right outside your door and was about to come in, but I thought better of it. You use very colourful language, I must say.'

He offered a smug smile. 'I was good, wasn't I? I was in great shape this morning. Feels wonderful to let it all hang out once in a while.' He sat down across from her. 'Great therapy.'

'Therapy for what?' The question came automatically, but she was sorry at once for her unthinking words.

There was a significant little silence as he gave her a long, meaningful look.

'Frustration. Rejection,' he said.

Uncomfortable, Faye looked away. Mrs Brown was rinsing her hands under the tap, dried them off and then took the coffee pot and filled Kai's cup. From the looks of it she hadn't been aware of their conversation, wouldn't have understood it anyway.

Faye looked back at Kai. 'Would you like some cake?' she asked in an attempt to change the conversation.

His eyes gently mocked her. 'No, thanks.' He drained his cup and put it down. 'Would you do me a favour?'

'What is it?'

'Would you edit my Nicaragua report? I'm taking it to Washington on Wednesday. If you could do it this afternoon, Judy Benton can type it up tomorrow.'

'Sure, I'll be glad to. I'll get started right now.'

'Thanks. But eat your cake and drink your coffee first.' He rose and strode to the door. 'I'll see you in a few minutes, then.'

What was she going to say to him? she wondered as she stood in front of his door once more. She'd have to apologise for her actions earlier that morning, explain ... Only she had no idea how to explain, because she didn't understand herself how it could have happened.

Having knocked, she opened the door and found him sitting behind his desk. She closed the door and leaned against it, fighting for composure. Now was the time and she wanted to get it over with. She couldn't ignore the issue, couldn't pretend it hadn't happened. She took a deep breath, and he looked up, his brows raised in question.

'Something wrong?'

'Kai ... I want to apologise for what I did this morning, and for what I said,' she blurted out. 'I don't know what got into me. I'm ... I'm sorry.' There was an unexpected wobble in her voice and she felt close to tears, for no reason that made sense.

Oh, God, she thought in sudden panic, don't let me break down! Please don't let me cry!

'Come on over here, Faye.' Kai got to his feet and pulled out a chair for her. 'Sit down.'

She did. With her head lowered she stared at the clasped hands in her lap. She heard him laugh and looked up in surprise. He was shaking his head at her.

'You sit there like a penitent little convent girl in front of Mother Superior.'

Sudden anger leaped up inside her. She was going to pieces and he was laughing at her. 'Go to hell!' she snapped, jumping to her feet.

'Good God, Faye, what do you think I am? I'm not sitting here in judgment over your moral values. I'm *not* thinking you're a lady of easy virtue, or that you offer yourself in that fashion to every man who crosses your path.' He gave a slow, lazy smile and his eyes were dancing. 'I have a strong suspicion that I was the first.'

Faye felt hot with angry embarrassment. 'Don't sit there and laugh! Don't you know how I feel? I feel indecent and cheap and. . . .'

'Don't blame me. I gave you a perfectly respectable offer.' Kai's face was expressionless.

Faye said nothing. The silence was uncomfortable and she was aware of his eyes on her, questioning. Then he sighed.

'I'm not shocked or scandalised by the fact that you took off your robe in front of me. What worries me is that I don't understand why you were so upset, what it is that's going on in your head.'

She didn't want to start the discussion again. There was nothing more to be said. She smiled thinly. 'Nothing much is going on in my head right now. I feel like a complete fool. And . . . and I just wanted to say I'm sorry for making such a spectacle of myself.'

'I'm not,' he returned dryly, and a glint of laughter was back in his eyes. 'You have a lovely body. Nice and smooth and. . . .'

'. . . full of scars,' she added, her voice toneless.

'Just on your stomach.' He paused and studied her face. 'You're not worried about that, are you?' he asked softly.

She hesitated, then shook her head. 'No, not really.' There were worse things than scars on your stomach, and didn't she know it.

'Good. Because to me it doesn't make a damn bit of difference. I don't want you any less because of it.' His eyes held hers, very steady, very calm.

A warmth spread through her and she licked dry lips. 'I think I'd better get started on your report,' she said unsteadily, and he took her hint and the subject was closed.

Faye took the report into Chuck's study, which was adjacent to Kai's office, and began to work. She was aware of Kai's presence in the other room, heard him move around as he talked on the phone. There were no more outbursts, but she could hear from the tone of his voice that he was talking business. Faye had noticed the difference before. With her he was gentle and caring and understanding, but when it came to business he was hard as nails and uncompromising.

It was after five when Kai emerged from his office. He said hello, sat down with the children and talked to them for a while. As usual Darci was the one who had the most to tell, describing in detail the events of the day, and anything else that came to mind.

'Auntie Faye is going to babysit us,' Darci announced at one point. 'Daddy's going away.'

Kai looked at Faye, one eyebrow raised in question. 'He is?'

'Just for the weekend.'

'Good for him.' Kai made no further comment, and directed his attention back to Darci.

Faye wondered about his plans for the evening. Would he ask her out to dinner? Take her home with him? They had spent a lot of time together before his trip to Nicaragua, but now everything had changed, whether she wanted to admit it or not.

Finally he said his goodbyes, taking Faye's hand and pulling her with him to the front door.

'Listen, Faye,' he said quietly. 'God knows that what I really want to do is take you home, but I'm not going to. Let's relax and play it by ear, okay?'

She nodded. 'Okay.' She felt strangely relieved. She wanted to be with him, still she knew she needed time to sort things out, get back on an even keel.

He took her face between his hands and kissed her, and it was a long, tender kiss and she knew without a doubt that he was telling her he loved her, because it was in the way he touched her, the way he held her. And when finally he looked up it was there in his eyes, too.

'Everything will be all right, Faye, I promise.' Then he was gone.

She saw little of him the next day, but her thoughts were with him every minute, or so it seemed. She was restless, knowing he was there behind that closed door, knowing she could go in if she wanted to, and she did want to, yet didn't. In the end she left the house and did the shopping for Mrs Brown, taking her time over it.

At four she brought him some coffee and he smiled at her and motioned to a chair.

'Are you avoiding me?'

'I don't want to disturb you unnecessarily, you know that,' she said levelly.

He grinned. 'You disturb me all right, whether you're in or out of my office, and in more than one way. You're in my blood.'

'Take two aspirins every four hours, lots of fluids and bed rest. You'll be fine in a couple of days.'

He gave an amused laugh. 'I'm not suffering from a

viral infection. My affliction is permanent and incurable.' His tone was light, but the underlying meaning was clear.

Faye smiled apologetically. 'In that case you'll have to suffer to the bitter end, won't you?'

He shook his head slowly, his eyes holding her. 'Oh, no,' he drawled. 'I don't intend to suffer. It will be sweet, very sweet.'

Faye looked away, and her heart felt like a hard tight ball in her chest. 'I'd better help Mrs Brown with dinner,' she said evasively, and he let her go, not saying another word.

An hour later he came into the kitchen and deposited his empty coffee cup on the counter.

'I'll be in Washington for a couple of days. I'll see you on Friday, okay?'

She smiled bravely. 'Fine.'

But he didn't come on Friday and she didn't hear from him until ten in the evening when he called her on the phone.

'I just made it home,' he said. 'I was delayed this afternoon and by five everybody in Washington was trying to get out for the weekend and I had to wait for hours to get on a shuttle.'

'I'm sorry,' she said automatically.

'So am I,' he said dryly. 'When is Chuck leaving?'

'In the morning. Nine or ten, something like that.'

'I'll come over and help you control the little beasts.'

'Thanks, I'd like that.'

There was an awkward little silence.

'Faye?' His voice sounded odd.

'Yes?'

She heard him sigh. 'Never mind. I'll talk to you tomorrow.'

She knew what he had been about to say. She knew it as clearly as if he had actually uttered the words.

And she was relieved that it had been left unsaid. She couldn't cope with words of love, felt a shattering sense of failure when they were said out in the open. If only he didn't expect of her a long-term commitment, if only they could go on without thinking about the future. The present was all that counted now, but obviously Kai didn't agree.

Saturday was a lovely May day, sunny and clear and bright. The tulips were out in colourful profusion, and creeping phlox decorated the earth in patches of white and pink and purple. It was a day for happiness, a day for fun.

The children decided they wanted to set up the tent in the garden, and Faye agreed to it, thinking it might be a good idea to air it out after it had been packed away in the attic all winter.

They were struggling with poles and canvas and ropes when Kai arrived, and he laughed and shook his head at Faye.

'Don't you even know how to set up a tent?'

She glared at him. 'Listen, I've never even seen this monster. There are no instructions, or even a picture, so is it any wonder I don't know what I'm doing?'

He grinned. 'I reckon not. And it's a relief to find you're not perfect at everything you try to do,' he said in a maddening slow drawl.

He shouted out some instructions, picked up a pole, and before long the tent was standing. The children were overjoyed, taking off their sneakers and diving inside.

'Can we sleep in here tonight?' Joey yelled. 'Please!'

'Absolutely not!' said Faye, sounding very stern. 'It's still much too cold at night.'

'Auntie Faye is right,' said Kai. 'No camping out yet. I'll take you camping again when it's warmer in a couple of months. If you're nice, though, maybe Auntie Faye will let you have a picnic here.'

Grudgingly they agreed to the compromise.

'I'll see what we have in the fridge,' Faye said, turning to follow Kai through the back door into the kitchen.

Out of sight now, Kai reached for her as she knew he would and she yielded to him as he drew her against him. He began to kiss her without any preliminaries as if it had been the only thing on his mind for days. Faye's response was instinctive and total and nothing in the world could ever keep her from reacting this way. She was drawn to him inexorably, with an insatiable need for his touch, a hungry longing she had never before experienced with any other man. Not even with Greg had it ever been like that.

It seemed an eternity when finally his mouth left hers. His eyes smiled at her in a brilliant blaze of blue.

'Oh, Faye, if only I could figure out what foolish thoughts are churning away in that head of yours!' His hands were playing with her hair, pulling at her curls, letting them bounce back one by one.

Faye freed herself, stepping back on unsteady legs. She forced a bright smile. 'Right now I'm mostly concerned about lunch—what to fix for this picnic we're going to have.'

Again he reached for her, taking both her hands, and he was no longer smiling. 'I didn't tell you yet, but I'm leaving again on Monday. I'll be gone for more than a month.'

CHAPTER SEVEN

THE words came unexpectedly, hung in the air like sudden dark clouds, threatening, cold.

Loneliness. It frightened her. She couldn't handle it any more, and it was a disconcerting thought. What had happened to her, to the self-reliant, independent person she had once been?

Kai seemed to fill her life, her thoughts, her very being. With him out of reach the days and nights loomed like a bleak eternity, an interminable blackness.

She glanced at his hands holding hers and she wanted to cry out, tell him not to go. Please don't leave me, she pleaded silently. I love you. I need you so.

But he would have to go. This was his job, taking on assignments in faraway places, coming back only to leave again.

She fought back tears. 'Where are you going?' she asked, her voice shaky.

'The Yemen.'

'The Yemen?' she echoed. It might as well be the moon. She couldn't even imagine how long it would take him to get there, somewhere half around the globe. The Yemen—a country somewhere in the south of the Arabian Peninsula, if she had her geography right.

'What are you going to do there?'

'Do a feasibility study for an agricultural project— upgrading farming techniques, irrigation systems, that sort of thing.'

'Are you going alone?'

'No. I'm part of a team of three. There's an agricultural economist, a hydrologist, and an agronomist, being me.'

Faye sighed. 'You wouldn't need a linguist, by any chance, would you?'

He laughed. 'Spanish and French won't do us much good out there, I'm afraid.'

Faye stared at his chest. 'A month is a long time,' she said bleakly.

'Too long. I wish I didn't have to leave. Not now.'

She looked up and saw his eyes. He was no longer smiling. 'Why?' she asked.

He looked at her ruefully. 'You know why—because of you. Because I want to keep you close at hand. I'm worried about you.'

Her throat felt dry. 'There's nothing to worry about. I'm fine. I'm perfectly fine.'

'Like hell you are,' Kai said roughly, then he fell silent, but there was something in his eyes that made her feel suddenly lightheaded and treacherously weak. He wanted to take care of her, and she wanted him to. Only she couldn't let it happen. She *had* to be strong. . . . Faye tried to free her hands from his grasp, but he didn't release her.

'Faye,' he said, 'will you wait for me?'

The question took her by surprise. 'Of course . . . I'm not going anywhere. I'll be here.'

'That's not what I asked.'

She stared at the buttons of his shirt, blindly. 'I'll wait,' she said huskily. For him she could wait for ever, only it was no use, no use at all, but he didn't know it and she couldn't tell him.

'Good.' He dropped her hands. 'Let's make some coffee and get started on that picnic lunch.'

All through the afternoon she watched him as he entertained Darci and Joey, laughed with them, played with them, and the pain inside her grew. She could not join them in their memories of last year's events—the trip to Disney World, the circus, and she sat silently listening, feeling the pain fading into a dull emptiness. He loved those children. He would make a wonderful father one day.

In the end she could take no more and she jumped up announcing she was going in to fix dinner.

'Hold it,' said Kai, taking her wrist. 'This is not a day for cooking. We'll go out. What do y'all want for dinner?' His question was mostly directed to Darci and Joey, and they jumped to their feet and cheered.

'Pizza! We want pizza!'

'Well, that's two out of four.' His gaze settled on Faye. 'And what would you like?'

'Pizza is fine with me.'

'I have an idea. Let's go to John's Best. The kids can have pizza and we can decide on something more sophisticated. How's that?'

'Fine.' She didn't care. It didn't matter. Her eyes flicked over the children. They were filthy. 'You'll have to wash and change,' she told them. 'I'm not going anywhere with you looking like that.'

They grimaced, and walked to their rooms, protesting loudly.

'Why is it that kids hate washing?' she asked half jokingly.

'It feels good to be dirty,' he returned dryly, and she looked at him in surprise.

He laughed at her expression. 'I grew up on a Texas ranch, remember? Sweat and dirt are a daily part of life, and you get used to it. When I was a kid I didn't like taking a bath, either, no matter how filthy I was.' He was smiling, memories alive in his eyes.

Some day, Faye knew, he would settle down in Texas, buy himself a piece of land—a spread, as he called it—and he would work in the sun and the dust and be dirty again.

She wouldn't know him then. It was part of his future she couldn't share. All this afternoon she had watched him with Darci and Joey, thinking of the children he would one day have, seeing in her mind the vision that haunted her. The low white ranch house under the bright blue Texas sky, the blond, blue-eyed children riding horses, the woman. . . .

Abruptly she turned. 'I'll get ready too.'

They had a nice meal and the children behaved themselves quite admirably, but then Kai had a way with them. Faye looked at him across the table and her eyes caught his and she smiled.

'Thanks for taking us out,' she said. 'Thanks for spending the day with us.' Of all the things he could have done with his day off, he had chosen to be with them—with her and two noisy children.

'You're welcome. I had to cancel the luncheon at the White House, but I didn't mind.'

It took her less than a second to catch on. 'I'm sure the President understands,' she said, face expressionless. 'He seemed like a very nice man when I met him a while ago.'

Kai grimaced. 'You're no fun. You're too smart.'

'Don't you like smart women?'

He looked at her through narrowed eyes. 'You wanna fight?'

'Have you seen my fingernails?'

He glanced down at her hands. 'I like smart women,' he said. 'Especially ones with long fingernails.'

'I thought so,' she said dryly. 'May I have some dessert?'

The children demanded attention. Kai scooped some tomato sauce off Darci's dress and told Joey to stop playing with the salt shaker.

We're like a family, Faye thought. Look at us sitting here, like thousands of other families having Saturday night dinner out. Oh, damn! Can't you ever stop tormenting yourself? Can't you ever just enjoy something without dragging past and future into it?

Apparently she couldn't. It was ruining everything, spoiling innocent, happy occasions like this one. Seeing Kai in the role of father was unbearable, and she would never get used to the silent pain that crept through her at the sight of him playing with the children; never get rid of that feeling of inadequacy—the feeling that she wasn't good for him, not good enough.

She drank her coffee, looked around the restaurant and watched other people. And to make matters worse Kai said he loved her and wanted to marry her. Kai. The most interesting and exciting man she had ever met in her life. Tall and strong, with gentle hands and the sky of Texas in his eyes.

Automatically she answered questions the children asked. Automatically she got up and put on her blazer, and they all marched out of the restaurant and scrambled into Kai's Rabbit.

At home she hurried the children through their showers and into their pyjamas. Kai had promised to read them a story, and it was getting late.

Twenty minutes later Kai came back to the living room where Faye was watching television. He walked up to the set, switched it off without a word and turned to look at her.

'Okay, my love, out with it.'

She stared at him, seeing his tall lean frame, dressed in jeans and sports shirt, the boots, the heavy leather belt around his waist. Legs slightly apart, he stood waiting, hands in his pockets.

'What's troubling you, Faye?'

She swallowed, her eyes on his face. He looked

tough and strong and very gentle at the same time. She longed to be in his arms and have him take care of her, wipe away her fears with gentle words and quiet reassurances.

But she was a woman on her own and she had to fight her own battles and overcome her own problems. Nobody could do that for her. Her life and what she did with it was her own responsibility and she couldn't burden anyone with that without losing her self-respect, her sense of self, her independence.

'Sometimes . . .' she said slowly, 'sometimes I feel like. . . .' Her voice had an undeniable tremor in it and suddenly she wished she hadn't said anything, because she could tell that the wobble in her voice had not escaped him.

'Sometimes you feel like what?' he asked softly. And the atmosphere in the room changed, and it was silent, very silent, with a waiting quivering in the air.

'Like . . . like I've lived a hundred years.' She felt old and tired and drained—weary with too many emotions she couldn't handle.

Three steps and he was standing in front of her, pulling her up and into his arms. Her cheek rested on his shoulder. She didn't move and couldn't speak.

'Why don't you tell me about it?' His voice was very soft and oh, so gentle, and tears welled up in her eyes and nothing could keep them back, and then she was sobbing, clinging to him. It was like drowning. Waves and waves of misery washed over her and she couldn't stop, and Kai wasn't trying to make her stop, but just stood there holding her quietly, waiting.

'Can't you tell me?' he asked at last.

'It hits me sometimes—depression, I mean. I . . . I can't help it.' Her voice was still thick with tears. 'I need a tissue. . . .' She moved out of his arms, found the box of Kleenex and blew her nose. 'I'll have to learn to handle it better, but it's hard.' She was looking, unseeingly, at a picture on the wall, her back towards him. He didn't immediately answer and when she turned around she saw the expression on his face and knew that the answer didn't satisfy him—not at all.

'Don't you think I know, Faye?'

Her eyes flew open wide. 'Know what?'

'That it's not as simple as that. That something's wrong, very wrong.' He paused. 'And it's got something to do with you and me.'

She was silent. There was nothing she could say. Nothing at all.

He looked at her calmly. 'If I didn't know you better I'd think you were still mourning your broken engagement.'

She shook her head sadly. 'I didn't love him. I don't love him now.'

'I know that,' he said, and he was smiling a little as he said the words.

'What makes you so sure?' After all, she could be lying, or pretending, to salvage her pride.

His eyes held hers for an infinitesimal moment. 'Because you love me,' he said.

Her heart began to beat erratically and involuntarily her hands clenched into fists.

'I never said that.' Her voice shook.

'No, not in words, anyway. And I'm well aware of that.'

Oh, God, she thought, I don't want to talk about this, I don't want to hurt him. I don't know what to do. She swallowed at the constriction in her throat and forced herself to look at him. She took a deep breath.

'I don't mean to disappoint you, Kai, but I . . . I can't give you what you want. It can't be what you want it to be. I'm sorry I keep breaking down all the time, but I can't tell you. . . .' Her voice trailed away. 'I'm sorry.'

'You don't trust me.' His voice was flat.

'It isn't that,' she said with a helpless gesture. 'There are things in my life that I have to come to terms with. Before I can share them or talk about them I want to get them straight in my own mind.'

'And I can't help?'

She looked away. 'No.'

He sighed heavily. 'All right, I'm not going to force you into an explanation if you don't want to talk.' He sounded tired. 'Our little talks always seem to end this way, don't they?' he asked bitterly, and the tone of his voice wrenched at her heart.

'I'm sorry,' she said miserably.

'Stop saying you're sorry, for God's sake!'

Faye thought her heart would stop and she stared at him in shock. Kai had never talked to her in anger, never shouted at her with such bitterness.

'Don't,' she whispered, 'please don't be mad at me.'

He jammed his hands into his pockets. 'Hell no, why should I be mad? All I have to do is take your word for it that what's between us is not going to lead to anything. I love you, but you don't want me to say it! You don't want to hear it! How do you think that makes me feel? And when I ask you why, you won't tell me. You're in tears half the time and you want me to believe nothing serious is wrong. Well, I'm *sorry*! I'm not stupid and I'm not particularly gullible. I have only a limited amount of patience and I'm human!'

Faye felt herself grow icy cold as his frustrated tirade washed over her. She wanted to flee from the anger in his eyes, but her feet seemed frozen to the floor. She watched him wordlessly as he picked up his hat, jammed it on to his head and marched out of the room. The door slammed and minutes later she heard the car engine start and he was gone.

She lowered herself into a chair, raised her knees

and hugged her legs. There was nothing but a bleak emptiness inside her and she stared blindly into space, feeling nothing, seeing nothing, hearing nothing. She couldn't think. Her mind was blank, empty. A numbness invaded her and she just sat there not moving, unaware of time until the grandfather clock shocked her back to conscious thought with its ten slow labouring rings.

Ten o'clock. She'd been sitting there for nearly an hour. Slowly she unfolded herself from her cramped position, grimacing at the stiff feeling in her muscles. She dragged herself to bed, making the minimum of her bathroom routine, going through the motions like an automaton.

She lay in bed, eyes tightly shut, but sleep wouldn't come. She lay awake while thoughts and emotions came flooding back.

Sooner or later she would have to deal with them. She couldn't forever slip into oblivion and ignore them. She couldn't hide from herself or from the reality that surrounded her, from the people who loved her.

Chuck was worried about her. He loved her. Her parents loved her. Kai loved her. How could everything be so wrong and so frightening when she was surrounded by care and concern and love?

Why hadn't she just come out with the problem right away—told her mother, told Chuck, told Kai? Then Kai would have known from the beginning how it was, what to expect.

But it had been impossible to talk about it, to tell anybody how she felt. She had locked away the knowledge inside herself as if it were a shameful secret. But she couldn't keep it there for ever.

The only one who knew was Greg, and telling him hadn't been difficult. Faye understood why. And the reason symbolised what had been wrong in their relationship. To Greg it hadn't made any difference, one way or the other, because it wouldn't affect his life. He had only looked at it in terms of himself, his own life. He had not seriously considered what it meant to her, how it made her feel.

Faye slipped out of bed and opened the curtains. Moonlight spilled into the room. Through the open window a soft breeze touched her face, the air balmy and fragrant. Tears crept into her eyes. 'Oh, Kai,' she whispered, 'I wish I knew how to tell you. But I'm so afraid.'

He would marry her just the same, she knew. He had made his commitment and he would never go back on it. But would she ever feel at peace? Would she ever feel that he wanted her no matter what? No.

She could never live with the doubt, the uncertainty, the sense of failure. She could never live with the fear that he would have been happier with someone else, a woman who could have given him the blond, blue-eyed children she had seen in her mind's eye—a family complete.

This evening he had left her in anger, and he had all the right in the world to be angry at her, she knew that and understood it, and she didn't blame him.

She didn't blame him. . . . It was the thought she eventually fell asleep with, and when morning came there was no more time for introspection; the children made sure of that. They ran around the house in their pyjamas, chasing each other, and finally collapsed breathlessly in front of the TV and watched Wonderama. Faye let them go ahead and went to the kitchen to mix up batter for waffles.

The morning dragged. The children became bored and went to play outside. Faye sat down with a book. She had made the beds, picked up clothes from the floor, hung up damp towels, loaded and switched on the dishwasher, wiped sink and counter and stove.

The house looked tidy enough. Staring at the pages of the book Faye waited, waited.

Kai would come and she knew what he was going to say. She wondered why she was so sure about him and it frightened her a little.

She heard his car, his solid footsteps in the kitchen. She rose from her chair and faced him as he entered the living room. His presence charged the air with a subtle, painful awareness. There was no anger in his eyes now and Faye wasn't sure what it was that she saw. He stood still for a brief moment, observing her silently. There was a solid strength about him, a calm, quiet determination—it was all there in his face and in the way he held himself, the way he looked at her. He wouldn't give up. Never.

They both moved at the same time, stopped with only inches between them.

'Faye, I didn't. . . .'

She shook her head very slightly. 'Don't,' she said softly. 'Don't say it. I know, I know.'

He looked at her gravely. Then he reached up and touched her cheek. Her heart contracted at what she saw in his face—the pain, the hunger. She closed her eyes and then he was kissing her, gently, very gently as if she were something very delicate and fragile and precious.

'I'll never hurt you,' he said softly. 'Never.'

He stayed all afternoon, sharing the simple mid-afternoon dinner Faye had prepared, telling the children stories of his childhood in Texas—a life so different from their own that they couldn't get enough of it. It was obvious from their comments and questions that he had told them about Texas a hundred times over.

'Have you decided yet when you're going back, Uncle Kai?' asked Joey.

He shook his head. 'Not yet.'

Joey sighed. 'I wish you did, 'cause I wanna come stay with you so you can teach me how to ride a horse.'

'Me too,' Darci said soberly. 'I can come too, can't I, Uncle Kai?'

'Of course you can.'

'Auntie Faye too?' Darci looked at him innocently.

'Of course, Auntie Faye too.'

'Maybe you can get married together,' she said matter-of-factly. 'You're always kissin' and huggin'. . . .' She glanced at Joey and burst out in giggles.

Joey shrugged and grimaced, obviously feeling himself miles above this silly little girl stuff, feeling it wasn't worthy of his reaction. Calmly he continued eating his ice cream.

Faye did too, determined to show no reaction and give no answer to Darci's question. She saw Kai's face, full of lazy humour, his eyes flashing blue lights at her, but she ignored it.

Darci had recovered from her attack of giggles and gave both of them a challenging look.

'Well, *are* you?' she persisted. 'Are you getting married together?'

Stoically Faye continued spooning in the ice cream.

Kai smiled at Darci. 'What do you think?'

She shrugged. 'I don't know.'

'I'll tell you what,' he said. 'When you do know, come and tell me.'

Darci's face clouded with frustration. 'You're tricking me! You're always tricking me!' She glared at them both. 'I know! You just don't want to tell me!'

'Right,' he said gently. 'It's big people business.'

'Daddy says that all the time.' Darci picked up her spoon and finished her ice cream. She looked deflated and disappointed.

'Very clever,' Faye commented as Kai helped her

take the dishes to the kitchen. 'But she wasn't very happy with the answer you gave her.'

'It was the best I could do. The other two choices didn't appeal to me.'

'What other choices?' She began to stack the plates in the dishwasher rack and didn't look at him.

'I could have lied and said no, and that didn't seem right. Or I could have told the truth and said yes and made you mad, and I didn't like that either.' His voice was calm, level.

Faye straightened her back slowly, turned to look at him. His face was expressionless. She moistened dry lips.

'You're very sure of yourself, aren't you?'

'I have to be,' he said softly. 'For your sake and mine.'

She didn't have to ask him why. He loved her, he wanted her, and he knew she loved him too. It was too important not to be sure.

Blindly she groped for the silverware and noisily pushed it into the dishwasher basket. He handed her another spoon.

'What time is Chuck coming back?'

It was a relief he didn't pursue the subject and she sighed deeply, straightening her back again.

'Around seven, before the kids go to bed.' She finished loading the dishwasher and switched it on. Kai began to wipe the counter.

'Would you like to go to a party tonight?'

'A party?' she echoed, and her mind produced memories of other parties—the parties she had gone to with Greg. Loud music. Smoke-filled rooms. People with phoney smiles plastered on their faces, drinking too much, laughing too much.

She didn't want to go to a party. She wanted to be alone with him. Tomorrow he would leave for the Middle East and she wouldn't see him for a month.

This last evening she didn't want to spend with him among strangers.

She hesitated. 'I'd rather not,' she said. 'I don't like parties very much. I prefer just ... just to go some place and be alone with you.'

Oh, why had she said that? It sounded like an invitation, and she had given him enough of those ... more than enough. And he had not taken her up on them. She knew it had been deliberate, but wasn't sure about the reason.

'I'd rather be alone with you too,' he said, and his voice was rough. 'You know damn well I'd rather take you home and lock the door behind us, but I'm not going to, so help me God!' He threw the sponge in the sink with a violence that unnerved her.

'Why?' she said, and her voice shook.

He looked at her with eyes that seemed curiously dark. His features were rigid, tight.

'Because everything is all wrong. And I want to get it right because it means too much to me.' His voice was very controlled as if he tried hard not to shout at her. He turned and strode out the back door. Faye watched him as he stood near a patch of tulips, looking down on them, head bent, thumbs hooked behind his belt.

She gave a deep, helpless sigh and walked out of the door and stood next to him. He didn't look up and she wanted to reach out and touch him, but didn't.

'Let's go to the party tonight,' she said.

He still didn't look at her. 'Okay, we'll do that.'

It was a big party, given by one of Kai's friends, a painter. The party was in celebration of his first major exhibition in New York. The whole atmosphere of the party was one of jubilation and goodwill, and against her expectations Faye found herself enjoying it. She had never seen a more colourful assortment of individuals, both in dress and in background. There was a blonde in an Indian sari who told Faye that she was an actress, after which she broke into laughter and explained she had done a commercial for laundry detergent. She eyed Faye curiously. 'Did you come with Kai Ellington?' she asked, and when Faye nodded she sighed regretfully.

'I used to go out with him a couple of years ago, but things weren't getting anywhere and I had to think of my career, such as it was.'

Faye looked puzzled. 'What do you mean?'

The girl grinned. 'Well, I need someone to support me while I try to make it in this business, and he showed no inclination towards matrimony, so . . .' She sighed again and didn't finish her sentence.

'You don't seem heartbroken,' Faye said dryly, and the girl laughed.

'A sense of humour is important, a sense of perspective.' Her eyes sparkled. 'I married a cartoonist six months ago, and he always says that.'

Faye laughed. 'Is he here?'

'Over there. The one with the beard and the bald head in the pink pants.'

Everybody seemed very friendly, very casual, and it wasn't at all like the parties Faye used to go to with Greg.

Greg. Chicago. It seemed another world, another time. And she didn't want to think about it any more.

They left the party shortly after midnight and the fresh crisp night air felt like heaven after the smoke-filled house they had just left.

'I met one of your old flames,' Faye said as Kai helped her into his car. 'The blonde in the sari.'

Kai groaned. 'Yeah, that one.' He walked around the front of the car and slid in behind the steering wheel.

'You don't seem to have damaged her heart permanently, though. She seemed quite friendly.'

'I try my best. I'm basically a very nice man,' he said smugly, and Faye laughed.

There was a silence then as they drove through the dark avenues and Faye felt a shaft of regret as Kai took the turn to Chuck's house. He wasn't going to take her home with him. He had told her he wasn't going to, so why was she disappointed?

'Would you like to come in and have some coffee?' She didn't want him to just drive off. She didn't want to say goodbye. She never wanted to say goodbye.

'Thanks, yes.'

Chuck had gone to bed, leaving the living room light on. He always did when she was out and she liked it. It made her feel welcome. It was depressing to come home to a deadly dark house.

Together they walked to the kitchen, very quietly, speaking in low tones so as not to wake anyone. Kai sat down at the kitchen table and watched Faye as she poured water in the coffee-maker and spooned ground coffee in the basket. She could feel his eyes on her, watching her every move, and a nervous quiver ran along her spine.

'It won't be long,' she said, lowering herself on to a chair across from him. He was still looking at her in a strange, hungry sort of way, and he was silent, saying nothing, just looked at her with those intently blue eyes. She felt apprehensive, jittery.

'Please,' she said huskily, 'don't look at me like that.'

'Sorry.' He shoved back his chair and rose to his feet, and crossed to the window. He stared outside, but it was pitch dark and there wasn't anything to see, Faye knew.

She stared at her hands, listening to the noise of the coffee-maker, willing it to stop. It did, at last. She stood up and filled the mugs. Kai came back to the table, sat down and took the cup from her.

'You can have my car while I'm gone,' he said. 'You still have the spare keys, don't you?'

Faye nodded. 'Yes, thank you.'

He took a swallow from his coffee. 'I'll leave it at the limousine stop. Chuck or Mrs Brown can take you there to get it some time tomorrow.'

The grandfather clock in the living room gave a solitary dong. Twelve-thirty. No, one o'clock. Kai came to his feet. 'I've got to go.'

She followed him into the living room to the front door. He turned to look at her and she went into his arms blindly. She lifted her face and kissed him with a desperate urgency, clinging to him. He groaned against her lips, pressing her closer against him. He answered her kisses with a fierce passion that left her shaking on her legs. The blood was rushing through her body like warm wine. She felt weightless and light-headed, barely aware that he was lifting her up in his arms. He laid her down on the couch, bent over her and kissed her closed eyes, her cheeks, her lips, in a wordless loving. She was lost in mindless emotion, feeling his mouth, his hands on her bare skin—sensing the helpless yearning in his touch, sensing too his love.

'Oh, God,' he groaned suddenly. He lifted his face and looked at her and she had never seen his eyes so full of wild longing. He moved away from her. 'I must be out of my mind! Next thing we know Chuck or one of the kids will come walking in here.'

The very thought was like a cold shower and Faye fumbled with the buttons of her blouse and stood up.

'I'm sorry,' she said bleakly, not sure what she was apologising for. She stood in front of him, almost touching but not quite, and he looked at her with an unreadable expression in his eyes. Then he touched her cheek, very gently, and her vision blurred. When would it ever end? This torturous longing that grew worse every time they were together, this endless yearning that found no fulfilment.

'Take me home with you,' she said huskily. 'Please take me home.'

'No, Faye, no.' It sounded as if the words were wrenched from him. He gave her a long, tormented look, then he turned abruptly and strode out of the house without a word of goodbye.

The night was endless, stretching interminably until finally a sunny dawn brightened her room. Faye dragged herself out of bed, through the shower and into some clothes. She barely touched her breakfast and Chuck studied her closely but made no comment. She was glad he didn't. She was in a terrible mood and might have blown up at anything he might venture to say about the way she looked.

The children went to school and Chuck left for work. Faye went through her morning routine of clearing the table and running the dishwasher, while she listened to the morning news with a half-ear. She made her bed and opened up her windows wide. It was lovely outside, radiant May sunshine throwing a golden glow over green grass and blossoming trees. Taking a couple of deep breaths, she calmed herself down, feeling anger and frustration fading a little.

There was so much in life to be enjoyed and she had to keep looking for it, remind herself that things could be worse. She thought of Kai, probably at the airport now, waiting to board the plane. Maybe things would turn out all right, maybe.

She didn't want to dwell on it. A month was a long time and she'd have plenty of time to think. Today she was going to do something to cheer herself up—buy a pair of sandals, a new swimsuit. One-piece suits were the style now, so she was lucky. With scars on her

stomach bikinis were not for her, but she didn't mind.
She didn't. She really didn't.

Two days later the long-awaited phone call from
Tom Finley finally came. With breathless anticipation
Faye listened to him talk. From the first thing he said
she knew that she had the job, and a rush of joy went
through her.

Secretly she had feared that she would be sitting
around the house for ever, doing nothing, waiting for
life to work its miracles all by itself. And nothing
would happen and then one day she would wake up
and find herself a bitter old lady, withered away, grey,
wrinkled, mentally dead.

A new job was what she needed right now, to keep
her busy, to keep depression away, to give her a sense
of worth.

The days passed. Faye started her new job and it
was all she had hoped it to be. It was exciting and
stimulating work. It demanded a lot of concentration
and consumed much of her energy. The days went
fast.

But at night other thoughts surfaced and she
struggled with her emotions. In her sleep she was helpless, victim to hidden memories and hidden hopes,
waking sometimes with tears running down her face,
her body curled up in agonising misery. Somewhere in
the deep recesses of her subconscious, she was still
fighting a silent, hopeless battle.

Then one day she came home from work and found
a letter from Kai.

CHAPTER EIGHT

A CURIOUS sensation stirred her nerves as she held the letter. Chuck put down his newspaper and she was aware that he was watching as she ripped open the envelope. Her hands were trembling and it annoyed her. She was sure Chuck would notice it and she didn't want him to see her go all nervous and jittery over a letter from Kai. He rose to his feet.

'Would you like a drink before dinner? It'll be another fifteen minutes yet before the food is ready.'

'Yes, thanks.'

'Sherry? White wine? Red wine?'

She nodded absently. 'Yes, please.'

'All of them, or just one.' He sounded amused, and she jerked her attention back to what he had said.

'I'll ... er ... I'll have sherry, please.'

He left the room and Faye sank into a chair and opened the folded sheets of paper. For a moment she saw only the large bold handwriting, strong and confident like the writer himself, and then it came into focus and she began to read.

'My Funny Freckle Face,' said the salutation, and it stirred in her an odd emotion. For the first time in her life she didn't mind being called freckle face. Coming from Kai it was somehow different. But then he was not an ordinary man, not ordinary at all. . . .

'My colleagues and I arrived in Sana'a yesterday and the town has not visibly changed much since I was here last, only this time I'm more lonely and my thoughts keep wandering back to you. I keep leaving you without saying goodbye. I don't want to say goodbye to you, ever.'

Chuck came in with a drink for each of them and she took the glass of sherry from him with a murmured thanks. Her eyes moved back to the letter.

'Last night I didn't sleep well since my biological clock hasn't adjusted to the time difference, and I lay awake thinking of you. I saw your face before me with all its different expressions—smiling, sad, serious, crying. I've seen you in so many ways, so many different moods and situations. I sense in you a strength, an independence, a strong determination. I sense in you, too, a sadness and a pain, a helpless struggle I do not understand. Many times I have watched you when you didn't know I was looking and I can see it all in your face, but the reasons elude me.'

The letter was quivering in her hand and she couldn't read any more. She laid the paper in her lap and carefully sipped her sherry. Chuck's paper rustled again and his eyes appeared above the edge.

'How's Kai doing?'

She swallowed. 'Fine.'

There was humour in his face. 'Why are you so shook up?'

She met his eyes. 'I'm not,' she said, and she could feel her cheeks grow warm, belying her answer. Damn, she thought angrily, why didn't I go to my room to read it?

Chuck gave a low laugh. 'Anyway, I'm glad he's doing his romancing by letter this time. If he has the gall to call you up again in the middle of the night, I'll think of a suitable way to torture him when he gets back.'

'Oh, get lost!' she said emphatically, and he burst out laughing.

'Emotions riding high, little sister?'

She refrained from answering, stuffed the letter back in its envelope and came to her feet. She would finish reading it in her room—without his help.

She made herself comfortable on the bed, leaning against the wall, the pillow at her back. She had not expected to get a letter from Kai, and certainly not a letter like this, with his feelings bare and exposed on the paper. Her eyes searched the words he had written.

'Faye, I wish you would trust me enough to tell me what's wrong. I wish you would understand what you mean to me, and that you would accept it and not fight it, as I know you do now. My love for you is not an empty promise, a temporary gift, or a passing fancy. I love you with an intensity I've never before experienced. It fills my thoughts, my heart, my soul, and all I can think of is you, and the very thought of losing you fills me with fear. You're everything I've always wanted, although I never knew what exactly that was until you came into my life. You have it all—the warmth and sincerity and humour and intelligence and that special magic something that defies description and that jells it all together and makes up the total red-haired you.

'I'm thousands of miles away and I don't want to be here. I've never felt like that before. I always enjoyed my work, the travel, the challenge. Now I know it has come to an end, this phase of my life. The time has come to make a new beginning. Everything is falling into place and taking shape in my mind—the future, my plans and hopes. And you are the part that made it all happen, that makes it all seem right.

'I know what you told me, but I don't want a temporary relationship. When it comes to you I'm greedy. I want all of you, a total life with you—the loving, the caring, the worrying, the sharing. I love you for a lifetime.'

Faye sat motionless, dazed by what she was reading.

She lowered the paper with trembling hands. It was too late, and if she needed any proof, it was all there on the paper, large confident writing spelling it out in blue ink on white paper.

All she had wanted was a lighthearted romance, a loose-end affair with a man known for his irresistible charm—Kai Ellington, the love 'em and leave 'em type. Only this time he didn't plan on leaving. 'I don't want to leave you, ever,' he had written.

'Auntie Faye! Auntie Faye!' The door was pushed open and Darci danced in. 'Daddy says dinner is ready. Please come and eat.'

The words barely registered in Faye's mind. She stared at Darci, unable to utter a sound.

'Auntie Faye? Are you all right?'

'Yes. Yes, of course.'

'You look funny.'

'I'm fine. I'll be there in a minute. Go ahead and start without me.'

Darci left, leaving the door open, and Faye focussed on the letter once again. There wasn't much more, but she was afraid to finish. She took a deep breath.

'Faye, I'm exhausted. I'm not even sure all this makes sense to you, but I love you, and that should say it all. I wish I could go to sleep with you in my arms. I wish I could see you now, feel you, hear your voice—and God knows I don't ever want to leave you again after this. I want you. I want you to be my wife. I want you to come with me back to Texas and help me build a life for us together. Be my wife, my partner, be the mother of my children. I can see them already in my mind's eye—red hair and faces full of freckles, smiling. . . .'

The letter slipped from her fingers and with an anguished moan she buried her face in her hands. Agony overwhelmed her, suffused her being, until all she could feel was an overpowering grief. She couldn't

cry. There were no tears and no thoughts, only a searing anguish and a hopeless sense of futility—feelings
too great for tears, too deep to be touched by reasoned
thought. There was no sense of time passing, no sense
of anything outside the suffocating sorrow that seemed
to drown her in its darkness.

A sound, a touch on her shoulder. Faye didn't stir.
Knees pulled up to her chin, face in her hands, she sat
rigid like a marble statue.

'Faye?'

Slowly she surfaced from the mindless darkness,
and the sound of her name registered, as did Chuck's
face. The dark eyes gazed at her in horrified surprise.

'What the hell is wrong with you?' The words shot
out in the silence, shocked her out of her stupor. She
lowered her knees and ran a hand through her hair.

'I'm all right. I'll come and eat now.' Her voice
sounded mechanical as if she were a machine.

'If you're all right, I'm blind and deaf and dumb!'
His voice was angry, but she recognised the worry and
the frustration in his face. He bent over, picked up the
sheets of paper off the floor, and Faye lurched forward
in sudden panic.

'Don't you dare read my letter!'

He handed her the letter, smiling in sudden amusement, shaking his head. 'You know me better than
that.' He looked at her intently, the smile gone. 'How-
ever, I couldn't help noticing. . . .'

'Noticing what?' She looked down on the letter in
her hands, the final page on top.

'His closing line. The words rather jumped at me.
"I love you, Kai." '

The words were there, in front of her eyes. She
swallowed. 'So?'

He sighed. 'A man tells you he loves you and you go
all to pieces. It doesn't make sense, does it?'

'Not to you, no.' She slid off the bed. 'Let's eat, the food is getting cold, I'm sure.'

'Dammit, Faye!' Chuck took hold of her arm and propelled her towards him. She stood in front of him, rigid.

'He loves me, yes. And I love him. So now you know.' Her voice was taut.

'I've known for a long time.'

'Good for you.'

There was a tense silence and it stretched as their eyes locked in wordless battle. Then, surprisingly, his face softened.

'Are you afraid, Faye? You think he might be playing games?'

'No.' She almost laughed, an hysterical impulse she checked just in time. If only Kai *were* playing games! She'd know how to deal with that. Everything would be fine then.

'He's an honest man, Faye. You can trust him, I promise.'

He stood there, looking at her with his dark eyes questioning, waiting for her to say more. But she remained silent, lowering her eyes to his tie, feeling miserable. He was her brother, he loved her, he wanted to help, and she stood there like an enemy, closed up, defensive.

He turned abruptly. 'All right, let's eat.' He strode out of her room and Faye's heart contracted painfully, knowing she had hurt him. She followed him slowly, distressed by the thought that she was hurting everybody who loved her.

She ate in silence, listening absentmindedly to the children's idle chatter, her thoughts with Kai's letter.

'I'm taking Darci to the doctor tomorrow,' Chuck was saying, and she looked up in sudden alarm.

'What's wrong?' She looked at her niece, who seemed perfectly fine, chewing peas and drinking milk.

'He wants to see her tonsils again. I called him about her noisy breathing. You said it was pretty bad that Saturday night I was gone and I've heard her again for the last two nights.'

When Faye came home from work the next day she was greeted by an ecstatic Darci. 'I'm going to have my tonsils out! I'm going to have my tonsils out!' She sounded as if she were promised a trip to Disney World.

'Maybe,' Chuck said dryly.

'What did the doctor say?' Faye asked.

'We'll have to see a specialist, an ear, nose and throat man. He'll decide. The pediatrician thought that her tonsils are abnormally large and could block her airway if she gets an infection.'

Faye sat down on the couch. 'I thought they didn't take out tonsils any more.'

'They don't often. This might be one of the exceptions.'

Faye looked at Darci. She looked too small to go through the ordeal of surgery. It would hurt—she'd be in pain for days.

'You're not afraid?' she asked quietly.

'She's gonna scream her head off,' said Joey.

'No, I'm not! Maybe you would, but not me, I won't!' The girl had spirit, Faye thought wryly. Maybe you had to, with a brother like Joey.

Outwardly calm, Darci made her trip to the specialist, and told Faye that evening that she did have to have the operation. She didn't care, she said, because she was going to eat lots of ice cream and she wasn't going to let Joey have any.

The next day Faye found another letter from Kai when she came home from work. She took it to her room and sat down on the bed to read it.

The envelope held a single sheet of paper and it wasn't a letter—it was a poem.

It took a minute to register the fact. Never in her life had Faye received a poem from a man. It gave her the strangest kind of sensation to think of Kai out there in the desert writing her a poem—a love poem. *Thoughts of You*, it was called, and with her heart in her throat, her eyes flew over the lines.

Loneliness and love and longing were expressed in the words hastily scrawled on the paper without much rhyme or rhythm. *Remembering tender moments, the silent eloquence of love, I long to hold you, touch your sad-sweet face.*

Faye swallowed, remembering too. A rush of longing swept through her, intensifying as she read the words of love that followed, a deep and urgent passion expressed in words that left her wildly flushed, the paper trembling in her hand.

For a moment she couldn't read on, overwhelmed by the knowledge of how vulnerable he had made himself, how totally and completely he trusted her by sharing with her the depth of his emotions.

She continued reading. It was a long and rambling verse, a collection of thoughts and emotions without much detail in form, as if all that had mattered was to put it on paper, to express his feelings the way they presented themselves.

In the emptiness around me I see your smile, the shadow of your fear; I hear your voice, a secret sorrow hidden in your words.

Her vision blurred, and she blinked back the tears. He knew too much about her, was too perceptive when it came to interpreting her moods and reactions. How was she ever to go on? How was she ever going to keep up this charade, this hopeless pretence?

She forced her eyes back on the paper, reading the final lines. *I long to hold you, quiet you with soothing touch. I love you so. Don't leave me out. Please share with me your love, your life, your sorrow.*

Faye was crying soundlessly, the tears dripping on to the paper, and for a long time she didn't stir.

Spring rain soaked the earth for the next two days, then Friday came with sunshine and temperatures in the seventies. All day Faye had felt restless. She had accomplished little at work and now she was home reading a magazine without any concentration. She felt fidgety and couldn't sit still. It was too quiet in the house and she didn't like it.

The children were in bed and Chuck had disappeared into his study to do some work. She didn't like being alone like this and it worried her. In Chicago she had often been by herself at night and it had never bothered her. She liked her own company and was never bored. But since the accident everything had changed. Now when she was alone she tended to sink into troubled thought and get depressed, so she tried to avoid it.

It was too quiet. A curious restlessness had taken hold of her. She got up from the chair and put some records on the stereo. Soft, quiet music filled the room and she poured herself an apricot brandy, then lay back in her chair and listened, her thoughts drifting back to Kai, as they always did. One more week and he would be home. One more endless, interminable week.

She tried to picture him at work, somewhere out in the Yemen desert, and failed. She closed her eyes, but all she saw was his darkly tanned face and the smiling blue eyes and nothing else—no desert, no other people.

The music relaxed her, soothing her nervousness. She sipped the apricot brandy, feeling its warmth spread through her, and a sweet drowsiness took hold of her. One more week. . . .

There was a quiet knock on the door and she heard someone come in, and when she opened her eyes and looked, Kai was there.

He stood by the door, not moving. Faye blinked, not sure whether he was really there. Was she dreaming? Was this some crazy trick of her imagination?

He took off his hat and took one step forward. 'Howdy, ma'am,' he drawled. 'Haven't we met before?'

For a moment Faye's tongue wouldn't move. 'You're back,' she managed at last, her tone low and incredulous.

A slow, lazy smile. 'Yes, I'm back,' he agreed. A few long strides and he was standing in front of her, pulling her out of her chair and into his arms. 'I couldn't stay away any longer . . . I had to come back.'

He kissed her and still she wasn't sure that this wasn't a dream, some kind of hallucination brought on by her yearning for him. It couldn't be real, this heady sense of ecstasy, this overwhelming sense of euphoria. But it was. He was here, really here, kissing her hungrily, holding her so close she could barely breathe. Every nerve, every cell of her body was reacting to his touch, and it was real, very real, yet in a way it was not. In a way it was still like a dream and she never wanted to wake up.

His mouth moved to her ear. 'You taste sweet,' he murmured.

'Apricot brandy,' she said promptly, and he laughed. It dispelled the dreamlike atmosphere and reality returned. And Kai was still there, very real, very solid.

'You smell nice too,' he added.

'Bath oil, soap, shampoo.'

'Mmm. Were you waiting for me?' he asked illogically.

'Yes,' she answered equally illogically. 'Of course.'

For a moment they stood silently in each other's arms, then she raised her face to his.

'When did you get back?'

'A couple of hours ago. I went home, unpacked, washed two days' travel off my body and went to bed. I was going to see you tomorrow, but I couldn't wait, I couldn't sleep.'

'You're a whole week early.'

A brief silence. 'I was worried about you. I had this terrible feeling you were going to walk out on me. I couldn't take it any more, so I worked like a maniac and got the hell out of there.' He tightened his arms around her and kissed her again with an almost violent intensity. 'Don't,' he groaned. 'Don't ever walk out on me.'

Faye's legs were trembling. 'I won't go unless you want me to.' It was true. She would stay with him until he didn't want her any more.

He held her away from him and looked at her with a deep, dark glitter in his eyes.

'Promise?'

'Yes,' she whispered.

There was a slight pause. 'Let's get out of here,' he said, and his voice sounded oddly husky, sending a strange quiver all through her body.

'I'll put some clothes on.' Faye walked to the stairs. 'And I'll have to tell Chuck I'm going out.'

'I already have. I saw him in his study when I came in.'

There was a light on in Kai's house, sparkling through the trees and bushes. There was a full moon and amid the tall, regal blue spruces his little cottage looked like something from a fairy tale—too romantic to be real. They got out of the car and Faye took a deep breath, savouring the sweet, cool spring night air, the spicy fragrance of the evergreens.

'It's lovely here,' she said in a low tone, afraid to break the magic spell.

'Would you like to take a walk?'

Faye nodded and he put his arm around her shoulder and guided her down the driveway on to the narrow winding road. They walked on in silence, a peaceful silence, but something was there between them, a feeling, a waiting. It was like a dream, Faye thought, feeling light and exultant, and it seemed as if it would never end, as if all this was for ever and ever.

They reached the end of the road and stopped. The moonlight gave a silvery shine to Kai's hair and Faye reached up and touched it and he drew her to him.

'It's a night for love,' he said softly. 'And loving.'

'Yes.' It was barely a whisper.

'I love you, Faye.' His eyes held hers and her heart quickened.

'I love you too.' She had to say the words—they were flowing over in her heart and they needed to be said.

'Oh, Faye,' he said in an unsteady voice. 'I've waited and waited to hear that. Was it so hard to say?'

'Yes.'

'Why?'

'I don't want to hurt you,' she said softly. 'I don't want to disappoint you.'

He hugged her convulsively. 'No,' he said hoarsely, 'you won't. You'll never disappoint me.'

Her throat felt dry. 'I read your letter, and your poem, and. . . .' She swallowed miserably. 'I can't deal with the future yet. Please . . . please don't ask me to.'

He didn't speak. His body was very still, very quiet against her, as if he had stopped moving altogether, stopped breathing.

'Kai,' she said softly, 'please kiss me.'

Without a word his mouth found hers and he kissed her wildly, desperately, in a kind of drunken frenzy that almost frightened her. Then he stopped, abruptly, breathing hard, and released her.

Slowly they made their way back to the house and in front of the door he stopped and kissed her again, very gently this time.

'Is this better?' he asked, stroking her hair.

Faye nodded, her eyes closed.

He lifted her face to his. 'Are you afraid?' he asked gently.

She looked at him and shook her head wordlessly. No, she wasn't afraid. Not of him, not of making love.

'I love you,' she whispered.

Without a word he lifted her into his arms, carried her into the house and into his room, and lowered her on to the bed. The bed, big enough for two.

CHAPTER NINE

IT was dark in the room and Kai switched on a small light and a soft warm glow spread through the room. He sat down on the bed and slowly began to take off Faye's clothes, his eyes on her face, then moving down to her breasts, her stomach, all of her. Warmth rushed into her cheeks and she knew she was suddenly shy of him, uncomfortable under his gaze.

'Don't look at me like that,' she said huskily.

He smiled. 'Why not? I love you and I like to look at you and touch you.' His hands roamed over her body in gentle, tender caresses, evoking sensual stirrings in her blood. She closed her eyes. And then it didn't matter any more, because what was happening to her now was beyond anything she had ever known, a sweet, sensuous delight she had never before experienced with such depth of emotion. Time stood still. She was floating, drifting, lost in feeling. An unexpected sigh escaped her, and Kai laughed softly in response.

Faye opened her eyes, saw him on the bed next to her, his clothes gone. He was leaning on one elbow, looking down at her, his other hand playing with her, touching, stroking, caressing.

'Magic?' he murmured, and then he lowered his mouth to hers, his lips brushing hers, kissing her with teasing slowness.

A restless urgency surfaced, heightened by his deliberate teasing, and she clung to him in a hungry response, overwhelmed by a primitive yearning.

'I love you,' she murmured. 'I love you.'

A quiver ran through his body and for a brief

moment he held her very tightly, then his grip slackened and his lips caressed her throat, her breasts, moving down to her stomach.

She caught her breath and her muscles tightened involuntarily, and in that instant everything changed.

'Don't,' she muttered. 'Don't. . . .' She tried to twist away from him, embarrassment and apprehension flooding through her. She didn't want him to touch and kiss her stomach as if nothing was wrong with it. She squirmed beneath him, but he held her down with the pressure of his body. His lips were warm on her skin, kissing her stomach, softly, gently.

'Relax,' he murmured. 'It's all right, it's all right.'

'No,' she said in a broken whisper. 'No, please. . . .' Her throat closed and no other sound would come.

He lifted his face, sliding his body up over hers to look into her eyes. 'I love you,' he said softly, 'and I don't want you to feel bad about your own body, or worry about what I feel or think about it.' He stroked back her hair, looking deep into her eyes. 'All I know and all I feel is that I love you, and nothing makes a difference. Certainly not some white and pink lines on your stomach.'

She saw the loving and the caring in his eyes, the infinite tenderness, and tears welled up, blurring everything. She averted her face and her throat ached as she swallowed.

'I'm sorry,' she said thickly. 'I guess I'm not really used to . . . to looking like that.'

'It's nothing worth crying about,' he said gently, one finger moving over her closed eyelids in a feather-light caress.

Nothing worth crying about. He was right. The scars in themselves were nothing. Why then did she feel so selfconscious at his touch? It wasn't rational.

No, it wasn't rational. And it wasn't so simple either. She turned her face to look at him and his blue gaze held hers for a long, quivering moment. Something in his expression changed, almost imperceptibly, and her heart beat against her ribs in uneasy rhythm.

'It's there again, Faye,' he said softly. 'I can see it in your face. What makes you hurt so? What is so terrible that you can't tell me?'

Her heart hammered painfully and she reached up blindly, pulling his face to hers. 'Kiss me,' she whispered desperately. 'Make love to me. Love me, just love me.'

'You know I do,' he said huskily. 'I'll do anything. Just don't leave me out, Faye. Don't close me out of your heart. I want to be part of you, part of everything.'

Faye longed to tell him, share her pain and disappointment, but fear of his reaction overwhelmed her. Not now, not now. All she wanted now was his arms around her, his kisses, his lovemaking, forget everything else.

Don't talk, she pleaded silently. *Don't ask me questions.* . . . The only safety was in that magic world of wondrous feeling where thought and reason didn't enter, where all that mattered was the thrill and excitement of the loving between them, even if it couldn't last.

And it couldn't. One day it would end, she knew that. But not now, not yet. This moment was all that counted. Her hands slid down his back and her mouth searched for his and she kissed him, fiercely, hungrily, until suddenly she stopped, aware of a change in him.

There was no response. He lay very still, his body rigid. Then, without warning, he released her and got up from the bed. He walked over to the window, picking up a robe from the chair, and opened the curtains. Outside there was nothing but the dark trees and a bright full moon.

'Kai!' It was a strangled sound. 'Kai, please. . . .'

'I'm sorry,' he said, his voice hollow, empty. 'I don't want it like this. I shouldn't have let it get this far.'

'Why?' she asked desperately, 'why?' Her whole body was trembling, hurting with a deep searing pain. 'Kai, I love you. Don't ... don't....' Her voice broke. Tears spilled over on to her cheeks and with an anguished sob she buried her face in the pillow.

'Yes,' she heard him say. 'You love me, but you don't trust me. You're holding out on me. You want to make love, and God knows I want it too. I want you so much, I've wanted you for so long, I'm going crazy.'

'I don't understand!' Faye lifted her face and looked at his back through a haze of tears. He turned around, his eyes meeting hers.

'If we made love tonight, what do you suppose is going to happen tomorrow night? And the night after that?' He took a step closer, his brown hands clenched into hard fists, the knuckles white. 'Faye, I'll be damned if I'm going to have an affair with you! I've had my fill of those open-ended relationships! I want to *marry* you! I want to wake up twenty years from now and find you next to me in my bed! Is that so hard to understand? I *love* you, dammit!' He sank down on the edge of the bed, took her shoulders and shook her. 'Why don't you want to marry me? What the hell is wrong with me, anyway? I earn a living, I pay my taxes, I shower morning and night. What the hell is it you want?'

His blue eyes were blazing into hers, and he was raging as if he would never stop. Faye shrank away from him in fear, huddled under the covers in utter misery, feeling his anger and despair engulfing her, choking her.

Oh, God, she thought, why didn't I tell him long ago? I can't live with this disappointment for the rest of my life. I can't, I can't....

'What do you want, Faye? What do you want?'

She closed her eyes and averted her face. 'Nothing,' she said. 'Nothing.' And then something broke inside her and a convulsive shudder shook her body. One sob followed another and she couldn't hold back. She began to weep, uncontrollably, covering her face with her hands.

'Oh, God,' he groaned, 'don't cry.' He gathered her up against him, his face in her hair. 'Don't cry, Faye. Don't cry.'

She clung to him, sobbing as if she would never stop. He said no more, just sat there holding her silently for a long, long time, until finally her tears were spent and she lay against him, trembling.

A drowsiness took hold of her. She didn't move. She had no sense of time passing, no idea at all how long they were just sitting there together, holding on to each other. Finally he stirred and made to move away from her, but she clung to him in sudden fear.

'Please,' she whispered, 'please let me stay here with you tonight. Hold me, just hold me.'

Next morning she awoke in his arms, aware with a rush of warm feeling that their bodies were naked against each other. A wild longing surged through her and she closed her eyes, huddling closer to Kai in blind instinct. She was aware of the warm male smell of him, the hard, muscular feel of his sleeping body against hers. Then he stirred and she knew he was awake. He kissed her closed eyes, and his hands touched her lightly, and in her still half drowsy state of mind she felt she was drowning. All she had to do was reach out and they would both be lost, but suddenly she wasn't sure that it was what she wanted now, not after what he had said last night.

'Good morning,' she said, opening her eyes.

'Good morning,' he replied, dry humour in his tone.

'I'm hungry,' she said, knowing the prosaic statement would take care of all sensual vibrations quivering between them.

'So am I.' There was irony in his tone, and she
knew by instinct that he wasn't talking about his
stomach, but she ignored it. She began to climb out of
bed and he let her go without trying to detain her. She
picked up her clothes and walked out of the room,
feeling his eyes on her back. She took a quick shower,
brushed her teeth, combed her hair and put on her
clothes. When she came back in the room Kai was still
in bed, hands behind his head, watching her as she
walked in. His expression was inscrutable, incomprehensible, and she stared at him for a silent
moment, confusion spreading all through her.

The blue eyes had a peculiar light in them, studying
her with a kind of critical fascination, as if she were a
stranger, as if he had never seen her before. She
averted her face, trembling suddenly, looking nervously for her purse. Her cosmetic bag was inside and
she fumbled clumsily as she took it out. Her wallet slid
to the floor, showering the contents of its sidepocket to
the floor. Credit cards, driver's licence, library card,
miscellaneous receipts. Muttering in frustration, she
gathered them up and stuffed them back in the wallet.
Then she got to her feet and left the room once more,
realising that Kai had said not a single word to her,
had been watching her with that strange look in his
eyes.

In the bathroom mirror she looked at her face and
began to put on mascara and lipstick, rubbing some of
it on to her cheeks to give them a touch of colour.
Nothing very special about her face. A lot of freckles,
yes. And he liked them, and he loved her. Strange, a
man like Kai who could have any gorgeous female he
set his eyes on. . . .

She snapped the cosmetic bag shut. She took it with

her to the kitchen. No way was she going back into the bedroom and have him look at her in that disconcerting way. She filled the coffee-pot with water and coffee and plugged it in. She heard Kai go into the bathroom. He was up.

Leaning against the counter, Faye stared out the window, seeing blossoming trees and a bright blue sky. It was lovely outside. All around the cottage were tall evergreens, contrasted by a big red maple, and several dogwoods, with white and sugary pink blossoms.

She turned from the window, poured some coffee and went outside. The air was clean and fresh, the sun warm on her face. The scent of pine trees was all around. She walked along the flagstone path to a rocky outcrop at the back of the yard and sat down. It was very quiet with only the cheerful chirping of the birds accentuating the peaceful silence. Faye sipped her coffee, her eyes catching a squirrel scurrying along the stone wall in nervous flight. It was nice here, a perfect morning, a perfect cup of coffee. Why was she feeling so desolate?

After a while she went back inside. Kai was leaning against the counter, a coffee cup in his hand. He had been watching her through the window, she realised.

'What would you like for breakfast?' he asked.

'Nothing much. A piece of toast will be fine. I'm not hungry any more.'

'Funny,' he said in a lightly mocking tone, 'I'm not either.' He straightened away from the counter, found some bread and put it in the toaster. His tall frame moved around the small kitchen with an easy, lazy grace. There was a pure, male sensuality about him and Faye watched him, an ache in her throat, a tightness in her chest.

Oh God, she thought, I love him so. What am I going to do? She swallowed, stood up abruptly and

took out butter and plates and put them on the table.
The toast popped out and Kai carried the pieces to the
table, buttered them and handed her one.

Facing each other, they ate without speaking. The
silence throbbed with tension, Faye didn't know why,
but she could feel herself grow tense with increasing
nervousness. Clumsily she pushed back her chair and
stood up to pour more coffee.

'Would you like another cup?' she asked, and the
silence was broken, but the uncomfortable atmosphere
remained.

'Yes, please.'

She filled his cup and handed it to him.

'Thank you.'

'You're welcome.' She felt like screaming. She sat
down again and looked at him. 'What's the matter?'

'I've been thinking,' he said slowly, his eyes holding
hers. 'A lot of things don't make sense and I'd like to
get something straight. You know what I want. But it
isn't at all clear to me what you want.' He paused,
searching her face. 'You told me you don't want me to
leave you alone. Also, you don't want to marry me.
How exactly do you see our relationship continuing
from here?'

She stared into her coffee cup and swallowed. Her
heart was beating in her throat. It took a moment
before she gathered enough courage to speak.

'I'd like to come live with you.' The words hung in
the air like a physical presence, alive with meaning.
She looked up and saw Kai's face, but she could not
make out his reaction. His face looked empty, devoid
of emotion. He said nothing. Faye swallowed again,
clenching her cup between her hands.

'I'd go to work in the city every morning,' she continued. 'I'd come home at night. I'll do my share of
the housework. I'll do your socks, if you want.'

The last remark was aimed at lightness, but it brought no smile, no reaction whatever. His face was inscrutable.

'I see,' he said slowly. 'For how long?'

'For as long as you want me.'

'What if I want you for ever?'

For a moment she couldn't speak. She closed her eyes. 'I'll stay,' she said.

Kai yanked his chair back and stood up. 'You're so damned generous!' The cold sarcasm in his voice shocked every fibre in her being. Never before had he spoken to her like that. She could feel herself begin to tremble and with an effort she controlled it.

'I'm sorry,' she said miserably.

He was silent for a moment, staring out the window. 'What about going to Texas?' he said at last. 'What about children? What about a family? How does all that fit in?'

There was only one thing to do to get through this conversation. Inwardly she hardened herself, grasping for every ounce of strength and composure.

'It doesn't fit in,' she said tonelessly. 'I don't plan on having children.'

He swung around and there was so much anger in his face that Faye shrank in her chair. He took one step forward, blue eyes blazing into hers.

'But *I* do!' The words shot out like bullets. Faye winced, her heart thundering.

'I know! And I'm sorry!' She couldn't bear to see his face any longer and she looked at the table top blindly. 'I'm not going to marry you. I'm not going to Texas. I'm not going to have children. So. . . .' Her voice trembled, but she took a deep breath and calmed herself. 'So, if you want to go to Texas and do your thing and raise a family you'll have to count me out. I'm staying here. You'll have to find someone else.'

Find someone else. Find someone else. The words

echoed in her mind and she wanted to scream out in agony.

'Why don't you want any children?'

She had been waiting for that question, knowing it would come sooner or later and prepared for the answer, coldbloodedly repeating it in her thoughts over and over again until no feeling would penetrate any more and the thoughts were cold, businesslike, unemotional.

'There are other things in life. I want to have a career and enjoy it without guilt feelings about my performance as a mother. I can't do it all, I'm not good at splitting my energy and attentions half a dozen different ways. I want to work in New York, learn Russian, make something of myself.' She gave him a quick glance, then looked away again. 'Motherhood isn't for everybody. It's not the only way to personal fulfilment.'

Oh, God, she thought in horror, listen to the clichés, the banalities.

'Is that why your engagement broke up? Because he wanted a family and you were not willing to co-oper-ate?'

She looked at him wide-eyed, speechless for a moment. Then a short, mirthless laugh escaped her. 'No, Greg didn't want a family. I told you, I didn't love him. That's why.'

There was an unnerving silence, vibrating with un-named emotion.

'But you say you do love me,' Kai said at last, his voice toneless.

'Yes.'

'But you won't even consider my side of the issue. You don't care a damn about what I want. Don't you think your terms are a little one-sided? Don't you think you're being selfish about it all?'

Faye didn't answer. One more word and she was

going to break down in tears, and she didn't want to
cry any more. She'd done too much of that and it had
to stop some time. Her jaws were clenched so hard she
wondered if ever they would unlock. She took a deep
breath and stood up, gathering the cups and plates and
carrying them to the sink.

Two steps and Kai was behind her, turning her
around to face him. His face looked grey, worn, as if
he hadn't slept for days. His hands gripped her shoulders, hard.

'But there's a reason for all this, isn't there, Faye?
Some crazy, wild, unimaginable reason. What you've
been telling me sounded about as phoney as a three-
dollar bill. You don't fool me for a minute, so don't
even try.' He paused and his eyes searched her face.
He sighed heavily. 'If we do what you say you want,
Faye, what do I get out of it? What's in it for me, in a
relationship like that? No commitments, no future, no
family. All I'm getting, Faye, is the privilege of your
company in bed.'

The privilege of your company in bed. Faye closed her
eyes and she could feel the strength flow out of her,
leaving her limp and shaking.

'Faye, look at me!'

She opened her eyes, stared at him blindly, not answering.

'Faye, I love you, and I want you in my bed, but
that alone isn't enough. For us it just isn't enough!'

She struggled out of his grasp and moved away from
him. She had to get away. 'I'm sorry!' she cried as she
reached for the door, wrenching it open. 'It's all I've
got to offer!' She flung herself out the door, ran down
the path, sobbing.

He didn't follow her.

The day passed without a sign of Kai. Faye wondered
what he was doing. Chuck was giving her odd looks

and every time she caught his worried glance she felt like screaming at him.

'Where's Kai?' he asked after dinner was over.

'I've no idea.'

'Is he coming here tonight?'

'I don't know.' She leafed through a magazine without looking at him. She heard him sigh.

'What's going on, Faye?'

'None of your business,' she said flatly.

'Oh, it isn't, is it?' He rose to his feet, slowly. 'We'll see about that.' He stalked out of the room and before she realised what his intentions were she heard his car roaring down the drive.

So he was going to see Kai, was he? Well, she doubted very much if Kai was going to tell him anything.

It took an hour, an interminable hour, before Chuck came back, and the expression on his face promised nothing good. He had her handbag in his hand and he threw it on a chair as he entered. She had left it at Kai's house and evidently he had found it.

Nervously she got to her feet, but Chuck prevented her from leaving the room.

'Sit down,' he said harshly.

Wordlessly she did as he requested. They might as well get it over with.

He towered over her. 'Now, let me tell you what I found when I got to his house.'

'I'm not interested,' she said coldly.

'Force yourself,' he said equally coldly.

Faye gritted her teeth and silence stretched between them until she couldn't stand it any longer.

'Well?'

'I found him sitting at the kitchen table with an empty bottle of Scotch in front of him. He was smashed.'

Fear shot through her, briefly. She forced it down.

Defiantly, she looked at Chuck. 'He's a grown man, isn't he? It's not my fault he drinks himself into a stupor. I'm not his mother.'

Fury leaped into Chuck's dark eyes. His face was rigid, his jaws clenched together. Faye could see the effort it took him to control himself and suddenly she was afraid.

'Let me tell you, Faye,' he said in a hard voice, 'just in case you haven't noticed, Kai is not the drinking type. He doesn't drink except for an occasional Scotch or a glass of wine. If he's drunk now, there's got to be a very special reason!'

'Did he tell you what?'

'No. But *you* will.'

She jumped out of the chair. 'No!'

He took her by the upper arms and looked at her with icy determination. 'I've never seen him drunk! Not in five years! I know you were with him all night and I intend to find out what happened, why he's in such a state!'

'I wish you luck,' she said caustically.

He shook her with a sudden violent anger. 'Will you stop the sarcasm? What the hell has got into you? Don't you know I want to help you?'

She wrenched herself free of his grip. 'I don't need your help! What's it to you, anyway? Why ... why don't you just leave me alone!' Her voice was unsteady, anguished. She saw his features soften.

'Because I care,' he said quietly. 'I know something's wrong. Why can't you just tell me? Why are you hiding behind all that anger and supposed indifference?'

Faye averted her face. Her heart felt heavy, like a ton of bricks suspended in her chest.

'Faye, please tell me what's wrong.'

She squeezed her eyes shut and her hands clenched

by her side. 'Leave me alone. *Please!* I can't tell you. I just can't. . . .' Her voice trailed away, trembling.

'Why not? I'm your brother. You've always trusted me. Why not now?'

Faye swung around. 'Because you'd tell Kai! That's why!'

He looked straight into her eyes, a very steady look. 'You know me better than that, Faye,' he said soberly. 'Whatever you tell me stays between us.'

Faye fought for composure. 'This isn't some innocent little kid's secret,' she said bleakly. 'If I told you, I know you'd feel obliged to tell Kai.'

There was a short silence. He looked at her with ill-concealed impatience. 'What do I have to do to convince you I won't tell him? Sign a contract in blood? Swear on a stack of Bibles?'

Her body felt tense, rigid, as if any minute now she was going to shatter into a thousand pieces.

'I can't marry him,' she said in a tight voice.

'Why not?'

'I can't live up to his expectations.'

'What the hell is that supposed to mean? He's hardly a romantic schoolboy. He's known a few women in his life and I doubt very much that he expects perfection from you.'

She gave an hysterical little laugh. 'Perfection he certainly won't get. You know what he wants? He said he wants to keep me in the kitchen, barefoot and pregnant.'

An incredulous look appeared on Chuck's face, then an impatient frown. 'And you took him seriously? He's not that kind of guy, you know that. He was leading you on.'

'Oh, yeah,' she said bitterly. 'I figured that. I'm sure he won't expect me to spend any more time in the kitchen than I want to, and I'll probably have a closet full of shoes. But I doubt very much that he was joking about the pregnant part.'

'So? Most men want children. What the hell is wrong with that?'

'Nothing! Nothing's wrong with that!' Her voice was raised in nervous pitch. 'Only I can't have any! I can't get pregnant, ever!'

CHAPTER TEN

A DEADLY silence followed her words. Faye stared at Chuck's face, seeing the stunned expression, the shock, and then the compassion.

'Oh, my God, Faye,' he said at last, all anger vanished from his voice. 'I'm so sorry. I'm so very sorry.' He reached out, drew her to him and put his arms around her. She leaned against him, suddenly limp and drained of all feeling and emotion.

'So that's why,' she heard him say. 'That's why all the tears and anger and depression.' The words seemed to come from a long distance and she didn't answer. He didn't seem to expect it.

He held her away from him and looked at her. 'It was the accident that did it, wasn't it? And all that surgery you had?'

Faye nodded wordlessly. She didn't want to talk about it. She didn't want to think about it. She'd come out with it, she'd told someone, finally, and in a way it was a relief.

'Okay,' he said decisively, 'let's sit down and talk about it.' He led her to the couch and sat down next to her.

'So,' he began, 'Kai loves you. You love him. He wants to marry you. Everything right so far?'

'Yes.' Her voice was dull and flat.

'But you don't want to marry him because you think he wants children.'

'I *know* he wants children. He's said so many times. All you have to do is watch him with Darci and Joey and you can tell how much he loves kids.' She looked down on her hands, swallowed at a constriction in her throat. 'There's no reason why he shouldn't have a family. There's no reason why he should suffer because of my inadequacies.'

Chuck let out an exasperated sigh. 'Good God, Faye, you should hear yourself talk! You sound like a character from some Greek tragedy!'

Anger surged through her. She jumped to her feet and glared at him furiously. 'Thanks a lot! Thanks for the sympathy and the help and your immeasurable understanding!'

Chuck stood up, slowly, and regarded her calmly. 'What do you expect he'll say when you tell him?'

'I don't know! I don't care! Besides, I'm not telling him!'

'Oh, yes,' he said quietly, 'you *do* care, and you *will* tell him.'

'No! And you can't make me!'

'Listen to me, Faye. You'd better think about what you're doing. If you want a man in your life there's no better than Kai. He's a man of character and integrity and loyalty.'

'Well, let him run for Congress! You sound like a damn political campaign commercial!'

He didn't reply to that, just looked at her with an unreadable expression. 'So you stayed with him last night and then you told him you couldn't marry him.'

'I told him I'd live with him.'

He looked at her incredulously. 'Nice, very nice. Spread out the misery a little.'

Faye clenched her hands into fists. 'Go to hell,' she said, and walked out the room.

She couldn't think clearly any more. She became aware of it as the weekend progressed. Her thoughts were chaotic and it seemed impossible to make sense of all that had happened. She wished she could put it all in order, understand it, but her emotions were master of her reason and paralysed her logic. It was like fumbling around in the dark, overcome by fear.

It was late Sunday afternoon and she had hardly exchanged a word with Chuck all day. They were out on the patio and Chuck was barbecuing a gigantic steak. Faye sat in a lounge chair and watched him disinterestedly. The table was set, the salad tossed, the dessert ready. She wasn't hungry.

It was warm. All around her the world was a rich luscious green and a soft breeze rustled the leaves. Why couldn't she enjoy it? Restlessly she stirred in her chair. All day Kai had kept intruding into her thoughts. Should she walk over to his house and make sure he was all right?

No. She wasn't going to do any such thing. He could take care of himself. He'd done so quite success-fully for many years. It was better, much better, to let things cool off.

Chuck turned the steak.

'When are you going to tell him?' he asked without looking at her.

'Why don't you mind your own business?'

'This is my business, Faye. You are my sister, and Kai is my best friend. You mean a lot to me, both of you.' He turned to look at her. 'I want you to tell him, because he has the right to know. Don't you know what you're doing to him?'

What was she doing to him? She closed her eyes and saw his face again—grey, weary. Her heart contracted and helpless misery washed over her. Oh, God, she thought, it's destroying both of us. It can't go on like this.

'I'll tell him,' she said with dull finality. It was in-evitable. Nothing else would do. Kai wasn't going to accept anything else. He didn't want her on her own terms, without commitment, without strings attached. *'For us it just isn't enough,'* he had said.

But what if they got married and went to Texas and he did what he wanted to do, turn the desert into food-producing land, would that be enough for him? No family. No children he could teach to ride horses, or to play the guitar, or to drive tractors. Would it be enough?

'Faye!' Chuck's voice broke through the cloud of thought. 'Faye, don't look like that! Tell him, please tell him, and it will be all right. He *loves* you, Faye!'

She looked at him blindly. 'Yes,' she said miserably, 'I'll tell him.'

'When?'

'I don't know.' Her voice was bleak. 'When the time is right.'

But the right time didn't come. Faye didn't see Kai at all for the next two days. Then Wednesday came, the day Darci was going into the hospital. Across the breakfast table Faye studied Chuck's face with apprehension. He was white and drawn, looking more like a patient than his daughter. Compassion rose inside her. As she sat on the train going into the city, feeling vaguely worried, her thoughts were with Chuck and Darci. She stared out the window seeing nothing of the passing landscape.

It had frightened her to see Chuck look so miserable this morning. Was he really that worried about Darci? She hadn't noticed anything special until today. He had been happy lately, quite obviously so. There was a woman in his life, Faye was aware of that, but she had refrained from asking questions and Chuck, as yet, was not talking. Chuck took his time, like always, making decisions with slow deliberation.

Not like Kai, she thought suddenly. Kai made up his mind quickly and then stuck with it.

She shifted restlessly in her seat, casting a quick glance around her. The other commuters were all hidden behind papers or magazines, or sat staring into space with blank faces. Nobody talked. Everyone seemed retreated into a private little world and ignored everybody else.

Tomorrow and Friday she wouldn't be on this train. Despite Chuck's protests, she had taken the two days off. The operation was scheduled for Thursday morning and if everything went well, Darci would be allowed to go home the next morning. Chuck intended to stay with Darci in her room and sleep there too, and Faye had thought that at least in the daytime she could take turns with him.

When Faye came home from work that night, she found Chuck in his chair looking washed-out and sick. Fear leaped up inside her.

'What's wrong? Where's Darci? Is she alone?'

'Darci is fine,' he replied. 'I just left her. She's in the playroom at the hospital, having the time of her life with the doll house.'

'What about you? You look terrible!'

He groaned. 'I'm coming down with something. I have a fever and I feel rotten.'

Faye stared at him. 'Oh, good lord!'

'The 'flu, or something. I have a headache and every bone in my body hurts.' He closed his eyes and leaned his head back against the chair.

Faye took a deep breath, gathered her wits and sat down. 'Okay, this is what we'll do. You go to bed and stay there. I'll take my night things and go to the hospital and stay with Darci. I'll be there when they get her ready for surgery and when she comes back. I'll take good care of her. Don't worry, everything will be all right.'

'Oh, God,' he moaned, 'I don't know. I promised her I'd be there.'

'She'll understand. And I'll be there. She'll be fine.'

He didn't answer, and she went up to him and touched his arm. 'Take some aspirin. Go to bed. Go on!'

With obvious effort Chuck dragged himself off to bed. Faye brought him aspirin, water and orange juice; asked him if he wanted anything to eat and he shook his head.

Faye called his parents-in-law and explained what had happened. Could Joey come over and stay for the night? Could someone come and check up on Chuck later in the evening?

Everything settled, Faye gathered some night things and drove to the hospital in Chuck's car.

She found Darci in her room watching television. Her small face lit up when Faye entered.

'Where's Daddy?'

'He's in bed. He's not feeling very well.' Faye sat down on the bed. 'Listen to me, Darci. I'm going to stay with you tonight, because I think Daddy should stay at home in bed. I think he has the 'flu and he shouldn't come here where everybody is sick enough already. Do you understand?'

Darci nodded, her eyes wide and worried. 'What about tomorrow? Will you stay with me?'

'Of course I will. You won't be alone, not for a minute. I'll just stay here and won't go anywhere, okay?'

Something in Darci's face made Faye turn around and her heart lurched. Kai was standing in the door-way, blue eyes meeting hers calmly.

'Hello, ladies!'

'Uncle Kai! You came!'

'Of course. I promised you I would.' He moved to the bed, hugged Darci and kissed her on both cheeks. 'So, Pickle,' he said in a lazy drawl, 'how're you doing?'

'I'm fine. I'm not sick, you know! I've been playing

in the playroom, and look, I've got my own TV! My very own, and I'm the boss of it!'

Kai laughed. 'Good. Enjoy it while it lasts.'

Darci threw Faye a quick glance, then looked back at Kai. 'Aren't you going to kiss Auntie Faye?'

'Sure I am,' he said easily. 'I just thought I'd find out how the patient was first.' He rose and came towards her and she didn't move. With one hand he lifted her face and looked into her eyes. Then he kissed her, a soft, gentle kiss. 'How are you?' he asked, his voice so low only Faye could hear it.

'Fine,' she answered automatically. It was a lie, and he knew it. She could tell from his face. His hand dropped and he turned to sit beside the bed again. He smiled at Darci.

'You're being very brave, I heard. Your daddy told me you didn't even cry when they took blood from your arm this morning.'

Darci looked pleased with herself. 'It did hurt though, but I'd decided not to cry, so I didn't!'

He stroked the dark hair and smiled, then looked at Faye. 'Have you had dinner yet?'

'No.'

'The cafeteria is closed, but we can get something at the coffee shop in the lobby, that is if Darci will let us go. If not, we'll take turns.'

Darci looked indignant. 'I'm not scared! I wasn't scared when Daddy went home, either! I'll just watch a show!' She fiddled with the TV, looking important.

'Okay, thanks, Pickle. We won't be long.'

In the coffee shop they ordered hamburgers and coffee and they ate without much appetite, making light conversation, carefully avoiding sensitive subjects. Like strangers, Faye thought suddenly, swallowing at a constriction in her throat. Picking up her cup, she took a sip of coffee, then forced down another bite of her hamburger. Staring down at her plate, she

could feel Kai's regard and when she looked up
something thrilled through her as her eyes met the
brilliant blue of his. For a fractional moment something quivered between them, a subtle awareness, a
knowing. Then Kai pushed back his plate, picked up
his cup and drained it.

'I'll come early tomorrow,' he said. 'I'll wait with
you while she's in surgery.'

'Oh, I ... you don't have to!' A rush of warmth
went through her.

'I know I don't have to,' he said patiently. 'But sitting here all by yourself for an hour just waiting is
hell.' He smiled. 'And maybe it will make Darci feel
better to know two of us will be here when she comes
back. With her only parent sick at home, she'll need all
the reassurance she can get, I reckon.'

Suddenly it all seemed too much. There was a lump
in her throat. His concern for Darci brought treacherous tears to her eyes and she blinked them away furiously. Why did it have to be this way? Why did it have
to be forced on her at every turn how much he cared?
A bleak desolation filled her senses. How can I ever
tell him? she thought despairingly. How can I ever tell
him he'll never be a father if he marries me?

His dark hand reached across the table and touched
hers briefly. 'Don't look so stricken,' he said gently.
'She'll be fine, and I'll be with you.'

Faye put down the uneaten portion of her hamburger. 'I can't eat any more,' she said thickly, not meeting his eyes. 'Let's just go back.'

Back at the hospital, in a quiet corridor, Kai stopped
suddenly outside an empty office, propelled her
through the door and closed it.

Bewildered, Faye stared at his shadowed features.
'What are you doing? We're not allowed in here!'

He didn't reply, just drew her into his arms and

kissed her. It was a very confident kiss, strong and warm, leaving her breathless and shaken.

'What was that for?' she asked, squeezing out the words between breaths, and a thrill of unexpected laughter went through her. This was ridiculous, standing here in an office kissing.

He laughed softly, pressing her close against him. 'To make you feel better, to cheer you up.'

'You're crazy,' she said.

'But it worked.' His finger outlined her lips. 'You're smiling. I like it when you smile.'

'So you got what you wanted—you cheered me up.'

'Right. I'm good at getting what I want.'

Her mouth went dry. With an effort she forced a smile. 'What did you do in college? Major in perseverance?'

He grinned. 'Right. With a minor in persistence. Graduated with honours.'

'I'm impressed.'

'Good. It's about time, too.' He lifted her chin and briefly touched her lips with his own. 'We'd better get back. Darci will be waiting.'

After Kai left later that evening, time stretched. Darci was too excited to sleep. The doctor had come in and asked her how she was, told her not to worry, and joked about the funny green suit he would wear for the operation, and the mask, and the hat. An orderly had rolled in a folded cot for Faye to sleep on, handed her a pillow and a blanket, and wished her goodnight. Faye couldn't sleep, was afraid she'd lie awake all night listening to the hospital sounds all around, remembering her own weeks in the hospital after the accident, and it all came back to her in a sickening reality.

Eventually she drifted off in an exhausted slumber,

and when morning came she was grateful. At seven a nurse came in to give Darci her injection. She knew all about it, Darci said. It was to make her sleepy. They'd told her all about everything when she'd gone on the tour last week, she informed the nurse proudly.

Kai came a while later, bringing in with him a waft of aftershave, a clean fresh smell in the stale, stuffy atmosphere of the hospital. Faye was glad he was there, glad he'd come so early. Darci was starting to be droopy, lying down on the bed, showing a distinct lack of energy. She was reduced to a sleepy bundle of inactivity when finally they came to get her, and Faye's heart contracted at the sight of her. She looked so small and vulnerable.

Faye kissed her on the cheek and Kai did the same. 'We'll be waiting for you, Pickle. Both of us, okay?' Darci murmured something unintelligible and then they wheeled her away.

'Come on, let's find some breakfast,' suggested Kai, and they went in search of the cafeteria, on the sixth floor of the building. Faye was hungry, surprisingly, and the food and coffee made her feel better.

Back in the room, Kai switched on the television to watch the rest of the morning news. He straddled a straightbacked chair, arms leaning on its back, and Faye settled herself in the easy chair next to the bed.

The news was depressing, filled with sorry tales of refugees and hostages, of poverty and starvation. There was civil war in one country, revolution in another. The price of oil had gone up again, so had the consumer price index. A small town in the South had been ravished by a tornado.

An involuntary sigh escaped her and Kai turned to look at her.

'I take it all this misery doesn't do a lot to cheer you up, does it?'

Faye grimaced. 'No.'

Pushing away the chair, he came lithely to his feet, and came to stand in front of her. He loomed over her, large and overpowering. Faye stared at the heavy buckle of his leather belt, overwhelmed by a mixture of emotions—love and fear and pain. She loved him. Why did it have to hurt so much?

Strong brown hands came out and pulled her to her feet, encircled her waist and drew her close to him. Her face was on his shoulder and the strength of his solid muscular body so close to hers filled her with a treacherous sense of safety. He wanted her. He loved her. He would take care of her. It was a dream, an illusion, a beautiful fantasy, but it was comforting while it lasted.

'They're halfway through,' murmured Kai in her ear. 'We can go and get another cup of coffee if you want. Or we can play cards. Or we can just stand here and I'll kiss all your freckles one at a time.' He moved her face and kissed her nose and Faye laughed.

'That'll take a lifetime!'

'I have a lifetime,' he said softly, and immediately she went rigid in his arms. She tried to move away from him, but he didn't let her go.

'Don't,' he said quietly, firmly. 'Don't keep pulling back, Faye. You can't keep running for ever, you hear?'

'I want to get some coffee,' she said, determined not to start another discussion. Evidently Kai didn't want to pursue the subject either, because he released her without another word. They left the room in silence.

They brought the coffee and some Danish pastries back to the room. The waiting dragged, and Faye was grateful for Kai's company. Finally the doctor appeared in the doorway, wearing a white coat over his green surgical outfit, and he gave them a reassuring

report. Everything was fine, he said, and it was all
Faye heard. Another hour in recovery and Darci
would be back in the room.

The white, moaning little girl who returned to them
was barely recognisable as Darci. For hours she lay
like a lump of misery huddled under the sheet. Once
in a while a nurse would come in and try to make her
drink something, and she would moan and cry and
Faye's heart contracted at the sight and sound of her.
She was given some orange medicine for the pain, but
all Darci wanted to do was sleep and avoid consciousness and pain altogether.

At lunch time, Kai went in search of food and
brought it back to the room for them to eat. A nurse
came in, gently woke Darci up and had her drink a sip
of juice. Darci swallowed, moaned, and went back to
sleep.

Faye finished her lunch and walked around the
room, stopped in front of the window and stared outside. She was restless and tense and had the begin-
nings of a headache. Kai came to stand beside her,
looking at her sideways.

'Why don't you go home for a while?' he suggested.
'See how Chuck is doing and tell him how things are
going here.'

'You don't mind?' Guiltily Faye had to admit to
herself that she was anxious to get out for a while,
breathe in some fresh air, feel the sunshine.

'No, I don't mind,' he said patiently. 'Go on, scoot,
skedaddle!'

Chuck looked horrible. He was still feverish and had
been in bed all morning. Mrs Brown was doing her
best to make him eat something, but to no avail. All he
wanted was some juice, and aspirin every four hours.

Faye told him Darci was still drowsy, but otherwise
fine, and Chuck gave a despairing groan.

'God, I feel like a failure! When she needed me most

I couldn't be with her.' He looked guilt-stricken, and Faye reached out and took his hand.

'It's not your fault—she understands that. And she's not alone. Kai was there last night, and he came early this morning.'

Chuck squeezed her hand. 'I don't know what I would have done without you two,' he said, managing a weak smile.

'Sure you do. Your parents-in-law would have taken care of everything. They're coming to see her this afternoon during the visiting hours, and they'll probably be back again tonight.'

He closed his eyes and heaved a big sigh. 'And all I can do is lie here and be sick. Some father I am!'

There was nothing Faye could do to make him feel better, but she knew it wouldn't last long. In a few days it would all have passed and both he and Darci would be fine again.

When she returned to the hospital she found Darci awake, sucking a red ice lolly, tears running down her cheeks.

'It hurts,' she whispered hoarsely. 'Oh, Auntie Faye, it hurts so bad!'

'I know, honey, I know.' Filled with a sense of helplessness, Faye stroked the dark hair. 'But it will get better soon, I promise.'

Darci was still groggy and she lay back against the pillow and drifted off to sleep once more. Tossing restlessly, she whimpered and moaned off and on. She woke up again when her grandparents came to visit, but she was too miserable to enjoy the toy they had brought her as a present.

It was Kai who really made the difference, and Faye was well aware of that. He read Darci stories, told her jokes and made her smile. With gentle persuasion he made her sip juice or water at regular intervals, as had been instructed by doctors and nurses. By evening

Darci had perked up visibly, even wanted to watch TV.

Straightening up in bed, she tugged at her hospital gown, frowned, and whispered hoarsely that she didn't want to wear that stupid thing. Obligingly, Kai pulled at the strings in the back and helped her out of it while Faye found one of Darci's own nightgowns in the suitcase.

She slid the gown over Darci's head and her eyes met Kai's across the bed. For a frozen moment she couldn't move, aware of what was in his thoughts in a flash of mystic communication. She knew it as surely as if he had spoken out loud. The knowledge and the feeling were there. The feeling of what it had been like that entire day, the two of them together taking care of Darci, worrying about her.

Faye lowered her eyes and quickly pulled Darci's arms through the sleeves of her nightgown and managed, somehow, to make some kind of cheerful comment.

Oh, God, she thought, the irony of it all. Look at us, playing father and mother to someone else's child!

She was overwhelmed, suddenly, by the need to get out of the room, away from Kai and the knowing in his eyes. She walked around the bed and crossed to the door.

'If it's all right with you, I'll go and get some dinner now,' she said to Kai. Her voice sounded strange in her own ears—strained, tense. 'Then when I get back you can go.' Not waiting for a reply, she turned and walked out of the room.

She took her time over dinner, chewing slowly, swallowing the food without tasting anything. Stress was starting to take its toll. She was exhausted, both physically and emotionally, and she forced her mind blank of thought, staring unseeingly at her food as she ate.

That evening Kai didn't leave until Darci was all settled for the night and Faye's cot had been wheeled in by an orderly. 'I'll come and get y'all in the morning,' said Kai as he left. 'Give me a call when you're ready to go.'

Mercifully, Darci slept straight through the night, although the tortured sound of her breathing kept Faye awake half the time. In the morning Darci awoke, whimpering that her throat hurt, but otherwise she seemed much better—more alert and less pale. She even had a few mouthfuls of jelly for breakfast, which was better than nothing. Faye's stomach felt queasy just looking at the sweet, slippery green stuff.

By twelve that morning Darci was settled on the couch in the living room with a concerned Mrs Brown hovering over her. The weekend lay ahead and Faye realised it wouldn't be easy. As the worst of the pain faded Darci would become more demanding and probably quite hard to keep happy. Chuck was still in bed, reading, feeling he'd better stay out of everybody's way so as not to contaminate anyone with his germs.

The weekend wasn't as much of an ordeal as Faye had anticipated, mostly due to the children's grandparents who came over to help, and by Sunday night Chuck felt better too.

Still, Faye felt washed out, and she fell asleep on the train going to work on Monday morning, something she never did. She had wanted to go to work, just to get out of the house and away from a tyrannical Darci, who now felt that she should be waited on hand and foot by everybody in sight. Mrs Brown was back on duty, so Faye had no compunction about leaving for New York. Work! Wonderful! Peace and quiet!

She took an early train home, feeling guilty about her escape, although she had worked hard and it could hardly be called a vacation. Kai was in his office and he came into the living room when she went in.

'Would you like a drink?' he asked, and she nodded gratefully, following him into the kitchen where Mrs Brown was preparing a light meal.

Kai took out glasses and poured each of them a drink, offering Mrs Brown one, which she laughingly declined. Handing Faye her glass, he gave her a probing look.

'How about going out to dinner tonight? A little bit of pleasure after a lot of hard work.'

'Oh . . . I. . . .'

'Yes,' Mrs Brown cut in, 'you do that. You need it. You look tired and it will do you good.'

'But Chuck. . . .'

'Chuck is fine,' said Kai with firm determination. 'We'll get the kids ready for bed before we go and he can do the rest.'

Faye hesitated. It seemed reasonable enough, and she did like the idea of going out and being served, instead of doing the serving as she'd done all weekend.

She smiled. 'Okay, I'd love to.'

Kai took her to a quiet restaurant and ordered soft shell crab for both of them. It was a delicacy, he said, only available for a few months in the summer. Faye had never had it before and when the food arrived she looked somewhat hesitantly at the crab on her plate. How was she supposed to eat it? she wondered.

'You eat the whole thing,' Kai instructed, 'claws and all. Don't worry, it's all very soft.'

It was delicious, Faye concluded after the first few brave bites. A little strange, but delicious. She thoroughly enjoyed the meal, and the quiet relaxed atmosphere of the restaurant. Nice wine. Flowers and candles on the table. Soft piano music drifting in from the bar. And Kai, smiling, making easy conversation.

A disquieting thought stirred in the back of her mind, then was lost. This was not the time to analyse their relationship, to sort out their conflicts. She wanted to enjoy this evening, not spoil it with disturbing thoughts.

She had expected him to take her home right after the meal, but he took the turn-off to his cottage and immediately the uneasiness stirred again, and stayed.

'I think I should go home,' she said in a tight voice.

'Everything's fine. You don't need to worry.' He glanced at her quickly. 'I just want to talk for a while.'

'We've been talking all evening.'

'There's something I want to ask you, something important.'

'No,' she said huskily. 'No.' Fear rose like fog inside her, clouding everything, thoughts, reason.

'Yes,' Kai returned softly. 'Yes, Faye.'

He stopped the car, got out and came around to open her door. She sat frozen in her seat until he gently pulled her out, and there was nothing she could do but let him take her into his house. And she was afraid, more afraid than she had ever been before.

She was sitting in a chair, filled with fear and a sense of inevitability, and Kai was standing in front of her, handing her a glass of wine. She accepted it and began to drink it, quickly, too quickly.

'Wait,' he said, 'don't hurry so. You have time.'

Time for what? She had the most horrible feeling that her time had run out. Gently he took the glass away from her and put it on the table. He pulled her up and she stood against him, heart hammering in wild, panicked beats.

'Look at me, Faye. Look at me.'

She did, and his eyes were blue, bluer than she had ever seen them before, like a bright spring day, a quiet, peaceful lake.

'Listen to me, Faye. I'm going to ask you a question, but before I do I want you to know something.'

He paused, moving his hands to her face. 'I love you,' he said softly. 'And no matter what it is you're going to tell me, it won't change it. Do you understand?'

She thought her legs would give away, and she was trembling, trembling. 'Chuck,' she whispered, 'he told you!'

'Chuck?' Kai's voice was incredulous. 'No, he hasn't said anything.'

And it was true, she knew, she could tell from his voice. But the shaking didn't stop, and his arms tightened around her, hard and strong, and she knew there was no escape. No escape from him, no escape from the truth.

'Faye,' he said softly, 'who is Doctor Jaworski?'

CHAPTER ELEVEN

FAYE could feel the blood drain from her face and for one horrifying moment she thought she was going to faint right in Kai's arms. The room tilted and everything swirled around in a wild madman's dance. She clutched at him for support, fighting for control, trying to focus at some point beyond his shoulder. Slowly, everything steadied.

'I ... I don't know him,' she murmured at last. 'I. . . .'

He reached in the breast pocket of his shirt, took out a slip of paper and held it out for her to see. One glance and Faye recognised it as the note from Doctor Martin with Doctor Jaworski's name scrawled on it, thickly underlined.

'How did you get that?' Her voice was a terrified whisper. She was still holding on, afraid she would fall if she let go.

'I found it on the floor in my bedroom. It must have fallen out of your wallet along with everything else on Saturday morning.'

Yes—oh God! Her legs were shaking so badly, she knew it was only his arms that kept her from falling.

'Who is Doctor Jaworski, Faye?' His voice was patiently persistent.

'I ... he. . . .' Her voice broke. 'Let me go, please let me go.' She felt as if she were suffocating in his embrace and she struggled against him, feebly, but it was no use.

'He's a psychiatrist, isn't he?' His voice was gentle, very gentle, and she looked up at him in stunned surprise.

He knew, oh God, he knew. She closed her eyes, a helpless sense of inevitability engulfing her.

'You know,' she whispered. 'How do you know?'

'Simple. Two minutes on the phone to Chicago.' He paused. 'Doctor Martin—was he one of the doctors who treated you at the hospital?'

'Yes.'

'Why did he give you Doctor Jaworski's name? Did he want you to make an appointment with him?'

'Yes.' Despondency overtook her. There was no going back now. No escape from the truth. No escape from his arms. Resistance faded and she felt numbed and lifeless. It didn't matter any more. Nothing mattered.

'Did you?' Kai repeated.

'Did I what?'

'See him—Doctor Jaworski.'

'No.'

'Why did Doctor Martin want you to see a psychiatrist?'

'I. . . .' Faye swallowed miserably. 'It's . . . it's therapy for grieving . . . mourning.' She made a helpless gesture with her hand. 'When people lose a . . . a wife, or husband for instance, they go through a more or less predictable pattern of emotions. . . .' She gave him a quick glance, then looked away. 'Like denial, anger. . . .'

'. . . depression, mourning, acceptance,' Kai finished for her, and she looked back at him in surprise.

'Yes.'

His mouth twisted in a little smile. 'I'm not totally ignorant about subjects other than agronomy.' There was a momentary pause as he scrutinised her face. 'Why did you need that kind of therapy, Faye?'

And then it was back again, the resistance, the revolt against his probing questions. She stiffened in defence—her whole body growing rigid with instinctive rebellion.

'It's none of your business!'

'Oh, yes, it is. We're talking about our life together. Your life and mine.'

She strained against him, hands pushing against his chest. 'Let me go! Please let me go!' Panic changed into tears. She couldn't take his nearness any more, the feel of his hard body touching hers, the strength of him.

'No, Faye, no. You're going to tell me. Now. I'm not letting you go until you've told me everything. Everything, you hear?'

'I can't!' she sobbed. 'I can't!'

'Faye,' he said slowly, 'you'll *have* to. You told me you love me, but you don't want to marry me. You have given me no satisfactory reasons, and I'll be damned if I'm going to accept your lack of explanations.'

'You have no right to demand an explanation!'

'Oh, yes, I have. You're part of me, Faye. Part of my life.'

'You talk as if you own me!' She was trembling, struggling to get away from him. She couldn't stand there, so close to him with all the pent-up despair inside her, the anger, the fear of what she knew not how to tell him.

His hands were warm and strong on her back, holding her steady. Then, with one hand, he tilted back her head and made her look at him. 'You gave me your love—I own that,' he said softly. 'True loving involves commitment, vulnerability, trust. Don't you trust me, Faye?'

New tears ran silently down her cheeks. 'If I told you,' she blurted out, 'you wouldn't ... you wouldn't. ...'

'I wouldn't *what*?'

'You wouldn't want me any more!' The words were wrenched from her in blind, agonising grief. 'You wouldn't *want* me any more!'

He shook his head incredulously. 'What makes you think you can make that decision for me? Do you have so little trust in my love for you?'

Faye didn't answer, couldn't answer. Through a mist of tears he was nothing but a blur in front of her eyes.

'What is so terrible that you can't tell me?'

She shrank inwardly, as if shrivelling away in pain. 'Let me go,' she whispered. 'Please let me go and I'll tell you.'

After a moment's hesitation Kai released her. Faye backed away from him, feeling like a terrified animal. She stood with her back against the wall, glad for the support, her whole body shaking. She took a deep breath and wiped her face dry with her hand.

'I'm afraid . . . afraid to marry you.'

'Afraid?' He looked perplexed. 'Afraid of what? Of me? Of marriage?'

Faye closed her eyes, taking another deep breath. 'I can't be what you want me to be. We can't have the kind of life you want.' She looked at him, standing only a few feet away, anguish tearing through her. 'I'm so afraid . . . you'll be disappointed,' she whispered.

'Oh God, Faye,' he groaned, 'I love you.' He came towards her and panic surged through her as he held her against the wall, his hands reaching up to catch her face between them.

'Don't,' she whispered. 'Please, don't touch me.' But it was no use. His mouth came down on hers and he kissed her with a hard, desperate passion.

'I love you,' he said huskily. 'I love you.'

Faye wrenched her face free from his hands. 'Don't touch me! Please don't touch me!' She was sobbing now, her words barely audible. Her knees gave way and her back slid down along the wall until she crumpled on to the floor, face in her hands.

Kai took a step backward and pulled her up. 'Stand up, Faye. For God's sake stand up!' He held her against the wall and she looked at him, seeing every line in his dark face, the intense blue of his eyes, and knew that this was the moment, that there was no more waiting.

And Kai knew it too. His eyes held hers locked in unrelenting demand. 'Why should I be disappointed, Faye? *Why?*'

Her heart was thundering in her ears and it seemed as if she couldn't breathe, as if she were going to drown.

'Because ... because I can't give you children! Because I can't get pregnant! I can't have babies! That's why!' Her voice was an agonised cry, torn from the depths of her misery. She yanked down his arms that held her locked against the wall and moved away from him. And then she saw his face.

It was ashen, grey under his tan. He stared at her as if he had never seen her before.

'Oh my God, Faye....' His voice was low and hoarse. 'Why didn't you tell me, why....'

Faye heard no more. She ran out the door, snatching her bag off the chair as she went by. The only thought in her mind was to get away—away from Kai and what was in his eyes.

She reached for Kai's spare set of car keys in her bag, doing it instinctively, knowing she couldn't walk home alone in the dark. How she managed to get the keys in the door lock and in the ignition she never knew. Somehow, she made it home.

The phone rang as Faye opened the front door and she heard Chuck answer it in the kitchen.

'She's just got in,' he said into the mouthpiece, smiling at Faye as she came into view. He listened for a moment, nodded. 'Okay, fine with me.'

Faye turned and walked up the stairs, taking deep breaths to calm her shattered nerves. Kai hadn't wasted any time checking up on her. She didn't care what he was telling Chuck, but she wasn't going to stand there listening to a one-sided conversation. But only a second later Chuck was behind her on the stairs.

'Kai wanted to know whether you'd arrived safely.'

'I did, thank you,' she said levelly, her voice surprisingly steady.

'I take it you ran out and took off with his car?'

'Did he say that?'

'No. He was *worried* about you. He wanted to make sure you went home.' He sounded impatient, and she couldn't blame him. She was making life unbearable for everyone around her. Everybody worried about her. Everybody loved her. Everything should be right. Only it wasn't.

'Well, I'm home now, and I'm going to bed. Good night.'

'Good night, Faye.'

Faye lay in bed without any hope of sleep. Mechanically she started to sort through her thoughts and emotions, preparing mentally for the next confrontation. There would be one, she didn't doubt it for a moment. But she needed time—time to clear her head, time to look at everything in a reasonable, unemotional way.

It was a temptation to run—get in the car and keep driving, but it would be a stupid thing to do. There was no place for her to go, and Kai would find her, no matter what. If there was one thing she knew about Kai it was his stubbornness and his persistence. She had to stick it out, right here, get it over with, deal with it. Only she didn't know how.

She lay listening to the stillness, just a few sounds here and there—the house creaking, a car somewhere in the distance, a dog barking. She had to think, but her mind refused to co-operate. She *had* to think, decide what to say to Kai the next time she saw him, but she couldn't think, she *couldn't think.*

And then, as she heard the door open in the silence, the quiet footsteps coming up the stairs, she knew it was too late, that time had run out.

Without even knocking he came into her room and walked over to the bed. She could feel the mattress sag as his weight came down on it. Her heart was pounding like a sledgehammer, and then his arms came around her and he drew her against him.

'Faye,' he said quietly, 'please marry me.'

'No,' she said thickly. 'No.' She could feel him stiffen against her and she released herself from his arms and slid off the bed. She switched on the light and stood near the window, far from the bed, far from Kai. 'I don't expect you to play the gentleman, I don't expect you to throw out a life of dreams just for the sake of chivalry. You don't have to marry me, Kai.' She barely recognised her own voice. It was like the cool calm sound of a stranger, unemotional, cold. 'You don't have to marry me,' she repeated levelly, giving him a steady look.

Her words were underlined by the silence that followed, a silence loaded with a strange, vibrating energy, a force in itself, filling the room.

Kai rose to his feet, slowly, and the face that looked at her was like that of a stranger, a dangerous, angry stranger. Never before had she seen him so angry, so full of hot, fuming fury.

'Shut up,' he said in a low, tight voice. 'Shut up and stop playing the martyr!'

The sound of his voice and the words he said shocked Faye into silence. She stared at him open-mouthed, and then a slow, burning anger rose inside her.

'How dare you! How. . . .'

He strode towards her and took her upper arms and shook her. 'Shut up and listen to me! What the hell are you thinking? What the hell did you expect me to do when you told me? You throw me a bomb and then walk out on me! What did you expect my reaction to be? Was I supposed to stay cool and calm and tell you it didn't matter? Would you have married me then? Well, let me tell you something! It matters! It matters to me! I am not apologising for my reaction!' He paused, breathing hard. 'You know I always wanted children, but what in God's name makes you think you're the only one who has the right to feel bad about it? I have that right too, you hear! I love you, dammit, and I want to marry you, and if we can't have children I have all the right in the world to feel bad about it!'

He stopped talking. He was still breathing hard and he looked at her with stormy blue eyes. Faye felt paralysed by his tirade and she stared at him, incapable of speech. She couldn't move, she couldn't think.

'Why do you think I want you for my wife?' he continued on a calmer note. 'Because you're some kind of baby factory? What kind of man do you think I am? I love *you*, not your procreating ability. So we have a problem. Well, we'll learn to deal with it, one way or another.'

There was another silence, and still Faye didn't speak, and she realised she was crying, soundlessly, tears slowly dripping down her cheeks. She was staring at his chest, blindly, not knowing what to think, not thinking at all.

He lifted her chin, gently. 'Look at me, Faye.'

She did, but his face was only a blur.

'Faye, we're in this together—you and I. Don't you see that? It's not just *your* problem, it's *ours*.'

'No,' she whispered. 'No!' She shook her head wildly. 'You have a choice, don't you see that? You don't have to marry me. You could marry someone else and have children of your own.'

'Oh, God, Faye,' he groaned, 'you're wrong. Don't you know? Don't you see? I *don't* have a choice. I never did have a choice, or a chance. Not since I met you and fell in love with you. I don't *want* anybody else, don't you understand that? I want you, only you.'

She wanted to believe it, give in to him. Never before had she wanted anything more desperately than she wanted to give in to him now. But she couldn't, she couldn't. . . . She closed her eyes, briefly, fighting for reason, common sense.

'Kai, I . . . I can't live all my life with your regret and your disappointment. Every time we see some pregnant woman, every time we're with somebody else's children I'll feel I've failed you! I. . . .' Her voice broke and new sobs came unchecked.

He held her very tightly until she calmed down and then he put her from him a little and gave her a dark, compelling look.

'It's not *my* regret, or *my* disappointment,' he said with quiet emphasis. 'It's *ours*. We're not talking about *you* or *me*. We're talking about *us*. I love you, and you love me, and that's the starting point, that comes first. From then on we're in it together.'

Faye moved out of his arms, away from him, but her legs wouldn't carry her and she sank into a chair. She covered her face with her hands and tried desperately to stop the crying, to stop the tears from coming and coming as if they would never end.

'How . . . how can I ever believe it?'

'Because I'm asking you to,' he said quietly. He
knelt in front of her, took her hands away from her
wet face. 'Look at me, Faye. No other woman can give
me what you can—yourself, your love, your warmth,
your sense of humour. All the facets of your per-
sonality that make up the final you. I've known other
women, Faye, but none of them have ever stirred in
me any feelings that come close to what I feel for you.
You're an original, remember? There's no replacement
for an original. There are only copies, and I don't
want a copy. To me you're special, and you'll have to
believe it, take it on faith. That's what love is all
about.'

He was holding her hands in his, strong brown
hands, and she was looking down on them, fighting
with herself, fighting with everything inside her to
believe what he was saying, to accept it, to give into it.

Leaning forward, Kai kissed her gently on the
mouth and smiled. 'It's all been too much too soon for
you, hasn't it? You never really got a chance to get
over the shock, and when I fell in love with you it only
made things worse.' He smiled ruefully and Faye was
surprised at his insight.

'Yes,' she said. 'It all happened too fast.'

'Bad timing. If only we could have met later, after
you'd sorted it all out in your mind, then it would
never have been such a crisis.'

She looked at him doubtfully. 'It wouldn't have
changed the facts.'

'No, but it might have changed your perspective.'

Would it have? she wondered. Could she ever feel
confident and secure in her worth as a woman? Or was
she at this moment too emotionally bruised to accept
that possibility?

'I don't understand,' he said, 'why I never guessed
what was wrong. Now that I know, it all seems so

obvious.' He looked at her thoughtfully. 'Faye,' he said gently, 'I want you to tell me exactly what happened to you, what Doctor Martin told you.'

She stared at him, surprised a little. A thought stirred in the back of her mind. Greg. He had never even asked. The why and the what had not interested him. But Kai, he wanted to know. She swallowed nervously and began the story, slowly, word for word, everything Doctor Martin had said. And he listened, quietly, not interrupting. 'So you see,' she said at last, 'we don't have to hope for any miracles either.'

'We'll make our own miracles,' he said, and smiled. 'Come here,' he said then, 'kiss me.'

She did, shyly almost, until he took over and lifted her up and carried her to the bed. He looked down on her, eyes thoughtful. 'I won't pretend I understand your feelings about this, the feelings you have about yourself as a woman, but I'll try.' He paused for a moment. 'Faye,' he said then, speaking with slow emphasis, 'don't *ever*, not for a single moment, think that you're not good enough for me. You're the best there is, Faye, the very best.'

His mouth sought hers and he kissed her with gentle reassurance at first, then with rising ardour. His hands moved over her body, touching her with sensual, intimate caresses.

'You're my woman, Faye, you're mine. . . .'

Her senses reeled. She could never love anyone like she loved him. No one had ever evoked in her this depth of emotion. This was real, this was for ever. Kai wanted her as much as ever. No chivalry, this, no game of pretence, she was very sure of that. And when he lifted his face and looked at her, it was all there in his eyes and the wonder of it filled her with joy.

'Do you believe me now?' he whispered huskily. 'Do you believe I love you and want you and need you?'

She nodded wordlessly, incapable of uttering a sound.

'And do you love me?'

Again she nodded, her eyes in his.

'Okay, then.' In one smooth flowing movement he got to his feet. He crossed to the closet, opened it and took out her suitcases. He put one on the end of the bed and began to pile her clothes in it, taking armfuls out of the closet.

Faye watched incredulously. 'What are you doing?' she managed at last.

Kai kept on moving around, opening drawers, taking out her things, filling the suitcase until it could hold no more. 'Get dressed. We're going home.'

'Home . . .?'

For a moment he stopped and he looked at her with a deep blue glitter in his eyes. 'Yes, *home*—where you belong. With me, in my house, in my bed, in my arms.'

'Oh, Kai,' she said tremulously, smiling suddenly, 'it's midnight!'

His eyes were very dark. 'I've waited long enough, I'm not waiting any more. You're coming with me, now. And I'm not letting you out of my sight until we're safely married. I don't want you getting any crazy ideas about running off to save me from myself, or some such notion.'

Her throat was dry. 'Please, let's not rush into it! Let's think about it first!'

Calmly he zipped up the full suitcase, swung it off the bed and put it near the door. 'I'm not rushing into anything,' he said levelly. 'I've wanted to marry you for quite a while, remember?'

He crossed to the bed, sat down next to her and put his arm around her. 'Faye, I wish you wouldn't worry so. I'm not going to change my mind. And I haven't shelved my hopes for a family, either.' There was a brief silence. 'When we're ready to have kids, we'll have them. We'll adopt them. There are orphanages the world over, full of children in need of love and care. We'll do whatever it takes. We'll get them, one way or another.'

Faye searched his face, faint hope flickering deep inside her.

'Would you want that?'

'Why not?'

'I don't know, really. I thought you . . . it isn't the same.'

'No,' he said levelly, 'it isn't. Adoption is a different process from pregnancy and birth, but the kids will be ours just the same and we'll love them no less.'

'Yes,' she said, 'yes.' And suddenly it seemed as if a light had been turned on inside her, as if suddenly she could see again, a future with Kai, a future with children.

A bronzed hand lifted her face. 'Look, Faye, I'll always be sorry. I'll always be sorry not to see you pregnant, not to see you with a big stomach knowing you're carrying my child, but I'll live.'

Faye lowered her eyes and tears threatened again. With both his hands he cupped her face.

'Look at me, Faye. I want you to stop thinking of yourself as a machine with a defect. You're not a damaged piece of merchandise, you hear? You're a living, breathing human being, a warm-blooded female, and I love you.'

Through a haze of tears she looked at him, giving a weak smile. 'I love you too.' She put her arms around him and he heaved an unsteady breath.

'Faye,' he said huskily. 'you're my first and only choice.'

CHAPTER TWELVE

KAI and Faye had their family, two girls and a boy. They came to them one at a time, from faraway places, with small faces and large dark eyes full of fear. In their faces Faye could read the tragedies of war and death and poverty. They were hungry for love, hungry for nourishment and care. At night they woke in terror, screaming, their memories alive in sleep.

Time passed, and in the low white ranch house under the blue skies of Texas they flourished like the crops in the fields. They grew tall and straight and healthy and the fear in the dark eyes faded. Like their father they wore jeans and boots and large-brimmed hats, and they rode horses and played the guitar. They learned to speak English with a Southern twang.

One day Kai and Faye watched them as they played in the garden, and joy and gratitude overflowed in Faye's heart. Life was good and filled with love.

'They're all ours,' she said. Even now after all these years she sometimes still couldn't believe it was really so.

Kai smiled at her. His eyes, still very blue, crinkled at the corners. 'Yes, and you're all mine.'

'They don't even look like us,' she said. 'Not even a tiny little bit.' No blondes, no redheads.

Taking her in his arms, Kai kissed her. 'They're true originals, like their mother. I wouldn't want it any other way.'

There was love in his embrace and love in his words and in her heart there was no room now for doubt, no room for sorrow.

Sometimes in the night he would reach for her and

she would wake to his touch, his hands on her breast, her stomach, searching. In the warm darkness of their bed she could come to him and they would hold each other close and she knew he had been dreaming.

She knew the dream. She was walking away from him, calling out that she couldn't marry him, the words echoing all around. *'I can't marry you! I can't marry you!'* And Kai was standing there watching her go, terrified, unable to move, his legs frozen to the ground. He wanted to follow her, keep her from leaving, but his legs wouldn't move.

Kai had told her of the dream, of the panic that clutched at him as he watched her walk out of his life. And always he would wake and search for her in the big bed, and she knew of only one way to reassure him. And in the warm afterglow of lovemaking, their bodies close together, she knew that to him she was everything, to him she was the only woman, beautiful, complete, whole.

Harlequin Presents...

The books that let you escape into the wonderful world of romance! Trips to exotic places...interesting plots...meeting memorable people... the excitement of love....These are integral parts of Harlequin Presents— the heartwarming novels read by women everywhere.

Many early issues are now available. Choose from this great selection!

Choose from this great selection of exciting Harlequin Presents editions

Relive a great romance...
with Harlequin Presents
Complete and mail this coupon today!

Harlequin Reader Service

In U.S.A.
MPO Box 707
Niagara Falls, N.Y. 14302

In Canada
649 Ontario St.
Stratford, Ontario, N5A 6W2

Please send me the following Harlequin Presents novels. I am enclosing
my check or money order for $1.50 for each novel ordered, plus 59¢ to
cover postage and handling.

☐ 99	☐ 103	☐ 109
☐ 100	☐ 106	☐ 110
☐ 101	☐ 107	☐ 111
☐ 102	☐ 108	☐ 112

Number of novels checked @ $1.50 each = $ _____

N.Y. and Ariz. residents add appropriate sales tax. $ _____

Postage and handling $ _____.59

TOTAL $ _____

I enclose _____
(Please send check or money order. We cannot be responsible for cash
sent through the mail.)

Prices subject to change without notice.

NAME _____
(Please Print)

ADDRESS _____

CITY _____

STATE/PROV. _____

ZIP/POSTAL CODE _____

Offer expires December 31, 1981.   104563170